A SPECIAL BREED OF WARRIOR

Joseph Mujwit

ISBN-13:978-1537680569
ISBN-10:1537680560

For R.A.M.

NAVY SEAL ETHOS

In times of war or uncertainty there is a special breed of warrior ready to answer our Nation's call. A common man with uncommon desire to succeed. Forged by adversity, he stands alongside America's finest special operations forces to serve his country, the American people, and protect their way of life. I am that man.

My Trident is a symbol of honor and heritage. Bestowed upon me by the heroes that have gone before, it embodies the trust of those I have sworn to protect. By wearing the Trident I accept the responsibility of my chosen profession and way of life. It is a privilege that I must earn every day.

My loyalty to Country and Team is beyond reproach. I humbly serve as a guardian to my fellow Americans always ready to defend those who are unable to defend themselves. I do not advertise the nature of my work, nor seek recognition for my actions. I voluntarily accept the inherent hazards of my profession, placing the welfare and security of others before my own.

I serve with honor on and off the battlefield. The ability to control my emotions and my actions, regardless of circumstance, sets me apart from other men.
Uncompromising integrity is my standard. My character and honor are steadfast. My word is my bond.
We expect to lead and be led. In the absence of orders I will take charge, lead my teammates and accomplish the mission. I lead by example in all situations.

I will never quit. I persevere and thrive on adversity. My Nation expects me to be physically harder and mentally stronger than my enemies. If knocked down, I will get back up, every time. I will draw on every remaining ounce of strength to protect my teammates and to accomplish our

mission. I am never out of the fight.
We demand discipline. We expect innovation. The lives of my teammates and the success of our mission depend on me—my technical skill, tactical proficiency, and attention to detail. My training is never complete.

We train for war and fight to win. I stand ready to bring the full spectrum of combat power to bear in order to achieve my mission and the goals established by my country. The execution of my duties will be swift and violent when required yet guided by the very principles that I serve to defend.

Brave men have fought and died building the proud tradition and feared reputation that I am bound to uphold. In the worst of conditions, the legacy of my teammates steadies my resolve and silently guides my every deed. I will not fail.

PROLOGUE
SAIGON, REPUBLIC OF VIETNAM, APRIL 29, 1975

Lance Corporal Rich Choatt peered down the street from behind the sandbags of his roadside checkpoint into the hazy air of the Saigon dusk. Irving Berlin's "White Christmas" played on a loop through the transistor radio by his side. It was ninety degrees and the humidity associated with the beginning of monsoon season in Southeast Asia was stifling. The North Vietnamese Army had Saigon surrounded and, after twenty years of U.S. Military involvement in the Indochina conflict, they were preparing for their final assault. Panic spread throughout the city. Riots broke out and there was incessant shelling on the outskirts. Helicopters continuously moved in and out of the area. No one in the military seemed to have a clue about what they were supposed to do and the young Marines manning the checkpoint were no exception. Their only orders were to cover the crossroads and not to let anyone pass who wasn't in a U.S. uniform. The incessant playing of a Christmas carol made the whole scene surreal.

At just nineteen years old, the Missouri kid was overwhelmed by his daily experiences in this strange country and the mess he came to know as Vietnam. During his eight months' tour of duty,

Rich was constantly in a state of confusion about whether he was loved, hated, or simply tolerated by the people of Saigon. Eventually, he decided that the easiest thing to do was to consider everyone a potential enemy. He hadn't had a good night's sleep since he was deployed. He joined the Marine Corps to fulfill a promise he had made to his grandfather who instilled in him a sense of duty and patriotism. Pop had convinced him that service to country was a moral obligation. Witnessing what unfolded before him, he began to doubt it.

Rich was part of a military police unit and trained to handle military working dogs at the Pacific Sentry Dog School in Okinawa. When he got to Saigon, he was teamed with his K9 partner Harley whose prior human partner was being rotated back to the states. Rich found Harley to be an excellent working dog and a great companion. It was only when he was with him that he could ever feel any relief from the constant stress caused by this morass of a military conflict. Rich formed a strong connection to Harley, who was intensely protective, but also incredibly gentle when given the opportunity to relax. He was a mix of German Shepherd and Labrador Retriever, which made for a great combination of dedication, courage, and intelligence.

Rich, Harley, and another Marine by the name of Corporal Sal Fasano had been given orders to watch the crossroads on the approach to Tan Son Nhut Air Base, the adjacent Tan Son Nhut International Airport, and the Defense Attaché Office (DAO) compound that was situated outside the air base entrance. As darkness settled on the city, the buildings appeared to be closing in on them and they knew they were being watched. They could see crowds moving, purposefully, back and forth across the street. Now the civilian population swarmed to form a mob, headed directly toward their position.

"Get ready," Sal said in an unsteady voice.

"Sal, how the hell are we going to stop them? They'll overrun us in seconds," Rich replied as he put a stick of Teaberry gum in his mouth.

"Let's fire over their heads and see if we can get them turned around. If that doesn't work, then we'll cut a few of them down to show we mean business."

As Sal was finishing his flimsy plan, a rocket slammed into a building a half block away. The sky lit up as the top two floors burst into flames and illuminated the street below, giving the three Marines a clear look at what they were up against.

"My God Sal, there's thousands! They'll be here in no time!" Harley stood up and took a defensive stance with his ears perked and shoulder muscles taut at Rich's side, ready to defend the post with his partner. He barked threateningly in an attempt to intimidate the advancing multitude, but the bedlam of the mob drowned him out.

Sal pulled back the bolt of the M60 machine gun and Rich tapped a magazine against his helmet to keep the rounds from jamming, inserted it in his M16 and flipped off the safety. As they took aim and were about to engage, a jeep careened into the street from the rear, kicking up stones and skidding to a stop beside them.

"What the hell are you two idiots still doing here!" screamed a gunnery sergeant from the jeep.

Sal shot back in rapid fire. "Gunny! What are we supposed to do? What's going on?"

"For Christ sake! Why do you think the radio is playing the same goddamned song over and over? That's the signal to evacuate! Don't you numb nuts pay attention to anything? Now I suggest you two *di di* out of here and get your asses to the DAO. That is, unless you want to be the last Marines left defending this shithole." Then the gunny peeled out leaving the three to fend for themselves.

"Asshole!" Sal screamed as the jeep sped away, "He didn't even offer us a ride!"

"Sal, we gotta get out of here."

"I know, I know. Let's try to get back to the DAO," Sal said as he snatched the M60 from its tripod on the sandbags and smashed it on the road, bending the barrel and rendering it inoperable. Then he picked up his M16, grabbed an extra magazine and said, "I'm not sure I know the way back through all this craziness."

Rich looked down at Harley. "Come on Boy, get us back."

The three Marines took off down the street, desperately trying to put distance between themselves and the steadily growing crowd. Harley knew the way. He had been in the city long enough to mark the territory between the DAO, the airport, and the checkpoint several times over. When he got off track, he picked up the scent of other military dogs and steered them down the street. As they made their way back, they could hear "White Christmas" still blaring from loud speakers throughout the city. The sound quality was awful and only made the entire situation more chaotic. As they continued to follow Harley back to the DAO, they encountered another small crowd looting a grocery store. When the group saw the Marines approaching, their desperation shifted towards the Americans and they began moving towards them.

"Stay the hell back!" Sal screamed at the crowd, taking aim with his weapon as they continued to come at them, undeterred. It was only when Harley jumped into action and took a menacing posture between the Marines and the crowd that they ceased their advance.

Taking advantage of the loss in momentum, Rich yelled "Let's go Harley!" and they took off down the street at a full sprint. After ten agonizingly long minutes on foot, they could see the lights of the DAO ahead of them. There was a crowd outside the front gate. The Marines and Airmen guarding it were barely maintaining order.

The three charged the gate, blazing a path straight down the middle with Harley madly barking and nipping at the crowd on either side. The guards saw them approaching the entrance and opened the gate just barely enough for them to squeeze through before slamming it shut again. As soon as they were in, the Airmen abandoned the post and the remaining Marine guards began wrapping chains around the cyclone fence gate, securing them with heavy padlocks. The crowd lurched forward, pushing against the locked gateway, and the entire fence line began to sway in rhythmic waves providing the only manifestation of order within the turmoil.

"Where are we supposed to go?" Sal said to one of the Marines who was placing the last of the locks on the gate.

"Sports court! Find any chopper you can! There aren't many left. We're getting the hell out of here!" Then he clicked the final padlock, turned, and sprinted towards the middle of the compound.

The DAO sports court had been turned into a makeshift landing zone. Two helicopters, both operated by Air America and piloted by CIA agents, idled there—a Bell 205 and a much larger Chinook CH47C.

"Which one, Sal?"

"I say we take the big one. It should have more room."

When they got to the Chinook, they could see that it was filled nearly to capacity. The pilot was standing outside the cockpit gauging the load of his human cargo, a mix of military and civilian personnel, to calculate how many more he could fit and still get off the ground safely. He was dressed in civilian clothes and wore a Boston Red Sox cap. However, his demeanor was every bit as military as the Marines loading up.

"Get your asses on board now!" he screamed at Sal and Rich as they charged toward the chopper.

"Come on Harley," Rich called to the dog. But just as they started for the helicopter hatch, a copilot suddenly stepped down in front of them, blocking their path to safety.

"You're not bringing that mutt on this chopper, Boy," the powerfully built copilot snarled in a deep southern drawl.

"The hell I'm not!" Rich snarled back, and attempted to push by.

The CIA agent, built like a bear and almost as strong, grabbed Rich, twisting him around in a hammerlock and pinning him against the side of the helicopter. He smashed his nose into the fuselage, and a stream of warm blood began to flow down the side of the aircraft.

Harley saw the attack on his master and lunged at the copilot, clamping firmly onto his left forearm. Rich screamed, "Harley, no!" in an effort to call him off, but the dog held steady.

The pilot reacted almost mechanically when he saw what was happening and drew his sidearm, taking point-blank aim at Harley. Sal, who had stood by confounded as the melee unfolded before him, suddenly snapped into action and charged, knocking the pilot's arm aside just as he pulled the trigger. The shot bounced off the makeshift tarmac. Undeterred, the pilot grabbed Sal by the throat and thrust him against the helicopter next to Rich, still pinned by the copilot who was unflinching, oblivious to the eighty-pound dog hanging from his arm, and the second stream of blood dripping down. The pilot kept Sal at bay with his left hand, reached across with his right, put the .45 caliber automatic up to the side of Rich's head and pulled back the hammer.

"Call him off," he spat at Rich, "or I'll spill all three of your brains on this court."

"Harley, release!" Rich called out.

The dog immediately complied with the command and let go

of the copilot's arm, backing off but still taking a defensive bearing ready to engage again at Rich's command.

Nobody moved and the pistol remained at Rich's temple as the pilot said slowly and with conviction, "He's not getting on this helicopter. Now, you make up your mind right now. Either you get on board without the mutt, stay here with him, or I put a bullet in you both."

"Pilot stand down!" A booming voice disrupted the standoff and the CIA agent lowered his weapon. Rich exhaled. "Does someone want to tell me what's going on here? If you haven't noticed, there's about a thousand Vietnamese out there about to reclaim this DAO."

The big copilot released his grip on Rich, and turned around to see an unamused Marine colonel addressing them. The pilot glared from under his Red Sox cap and spoke up, "He can't take the dog on this chopper, Colonel."

The colonel looked back at the pilot and nodded his agreement.

"Corporal," he said to Sal, "Go ahead and get on board. Lance Corporal, come with me." Then he turned back to the chopper pilot. "Make preparations to get underway, we'll be with you in a minute. And get a corpsman to look at that man's arm."

The colonel motioned for Rich to walk with him and pulled a red bandanna from his pocket, pointing to Rich's still-bleeding nose. Rich signaled and Harley fell in behind them.

"Son," he said to Rich in a compassionate tone as he put his arm over his shoulder and guided him away from the noise of the helicopter, "He can't come with us. We are loaded to capacity and we have a dozen orphans on board."

"But Colonel, we can't just leave him! We've been together since I got here. He's a good dog and won't make any problems. I promise. Please, Sir."

"None of them are going back," the colonel said. "We're leaving the military dogs behind. All of them. I understand how you feel. I have one just like him at home. Now he's done his job and his duty is complete, but he has to stay. Now, go on and get on board."

Rich opened his mouth to speak again but he knew any further attempts to change the colonel's mind would be futile. The colonel strode toward the waiting helicopters and Rich bent down on one knee in front of Harley.

"You're a good boy. Thank you," he said, holding the dog's head in his hands and rubbing him behind his ears. "Now you sit here." Then Rich dug out the last dog biscuit he had in his pocket and put it in his mouth, the end dangling as if he was puffing a cigar. Harley hesitantly took the biscuit from him, but didn't bite down. "Now you be a good boy and stay," Rich said. Then he backed his way to the helicopter, the last to board.

As soon as Rich stepped into the chopper and stowed the stairway, the sound of the engines intensified and the aircraft began lifting from the ground. As he looked down, he saw Harley starting to shiver, gazing back up at him as if waiting for his next command, with the biscuit still hanging from his muzzle. Rich glanced over to the fence line and gate, now breached as the panicked crowd poured into the DAO. Even as the Vietnamese spilled onto the sports court, Harley remained motionless, staring up at Rich with his ears collapsed to the side of his head. Rich could see the look of fear and confusion in his eyes and knew he was silently imploring Rich to come back for him. Then the electricity went out in the entire DAO and only the spotlights from the fleeing airborne armada passed over the compound. Rich stared down through the darting beams of light and caught one last glimpse of Harley before the throng filled the court and engulfed him. He was gone.

When Rich could no longer make out the compound, he looked up to see what seemed like an endless line of helicopters. They were heading out to sea for waiting aircraft carriers. The sky looked like it was filled with fireflies as the largest airlift in history completed its final stages.

Thirty minutes later, the helicopter landed on the deck of the U.S.S. Midway. Rich was the first one out. He stood and watched as everyone was taken off and moved below decks to have their medical needs evaluated. As the last passengers left the helicopter, the Marine colonel who intervened at the DAO approached him and lit a cigarette.

"That's a hell of an aircraft, isn't it Marine?" The colonel asked rhetorically. "It flew us all the way out here and probably saved our lives."

Rich didn't respond, but stared past him as about thirty Sailors approached the helicopter and began rolling it to the side of the flight deck. When they got to the edge they didn't stop, instead exerting even more effort as the wheels kept rolling and the chopper picked up speed. The Sailors proceeded to push the machine right off the end of the deck and into the South China Sea. Rich ran to the end of the flight deck and watched as the Chinook bobbed on the surface for a minute before finally sinking as the open compartments filled with salt water. Then he turned and looked up at the colonel, dumbfounded by what he had just seen.

The colonel was watching Rich and, as if reading his mind, said, "We don't have room for it. There's more choppers coming and we need to keep this flight deck clear. We dumped millions of dollars' worth of valuable military armaments into that sea tonight and left millions more back on land. It is a regrettable waste of equipment. But do you know something? We saved a hell of a lot of people over the last two days." He paused for a moment and continued, "You did a good job tonight son. You made a difficult decision but you did your job and you're going home alive—which is more than I can say for a lot of other Marines."

Then he dropped the cigarette, snuffed it out with his boot, and left Rich alone to stare out at the lights of the other ships and more helicopters making their approaches.

Rich took no consolation in the colonel's words. From that day forward, he would fall into a deep depression during the holidays and become physically ill whenever he heard "White Christmas."

Chapter 1
A Special Breed of Warrior

Shadow bounded through the Florida panhandle brush and grass field homing in on her prize. The black lab moved purposefully through the scrub, examining the various debris and makeshift shelters placed throughout the training grounds of Facility Range D-4 at Eglin Air Force Base. At times, only the tip of her ebony tail was visible above the greenish tan plants and looked like a periscope knifing through the swaying vegetation in the late afternoon breeze.

She didn't realize it but Shadow was in a race. Across the field, an explosive ordnance disposal technician was searching for the same target. Somewhere on the grounds was a brick of Semtex plastic explosive like the kind used by terrorists to bring down Pan Am Flight 103 over Lockerbie, Scotland. He was carrying a boxy device about the size of a six pack with a flexible hose attached to a rigid stainless steel tube. As he swept the tube back and forth, he watched the analog gauge's needle bounce up and down as it detected the varying concentration of nitrates in the air.

It turned out not to be much of a race. Within a few minutes, Shadow came upon a rusty old military truck. She circled it one time and then stopped at the spare tire mounted on the back. She took a seat and waited to be called back. The EOD tech saw Shadow sit down, and knowing he was beat, threw his hands up in frustration.

"Heh, Heh," Rich chuckled as he unwrapped a stick of Teaberry. "What's the score now?"

"You know the score. You don't have to rub it in," said the professor standing in the bed of Rich's pickup truck next to him. He watched Rich chomping on the gum, "Teaberry? Do they still make that?"

"Yeah, I know the score," Rich said. "And yes they do. I have a connection." He adjusted his International Harvester baseball cap while grinning in triumph. His gray hair and mature features accentuated in the orange glow of the setting sun.

"Look," Rich continued, "the technology simply isn't there yet. I hear they are working with lasers now or something. Dogs are still just better at explosive detection—especially in the field. Shadow isn't even my best and she beats your *toy* 80 percent of the time. How much did that thing cost anyway?"

"It's a prototype. They always cost more."

"Uh huh, how much?"

"This one is about three quarters of a million."

Rich nearly spit his gum out. "Dollars?"

The professor looked back at him and sheepishly nodded.

As Rich needled the professor, an Army lieutenant general approached them with the EOD technician by his side. He rested his arms on the edge of the truck bed and looked up at the two.

"Well Professor Bonetti, it looks like we still aren't there yet."

"General, why do you keep trying?" Rich asked. "These dogs are efficient, obedient; they don't require a lot of maintenance…"

The general cut him off. "I know Mr. Choatt. We've been through all that. The Defense Advanced Research Projects Agency and JIEDDO are funding this and they have decided to keep working on a mechanical alternative."

"I'm sorry General, I understand. It's just that we could have trained and equipped an awful lot of dogs for the $19 billion already spent to develop this technology."

"I have to say, I agree with you on that. As head of the Joint

Improvised Explosive Detection and Defeat Organization, I have been tasked to keep moving on this and to explore all the best options. The Taliban and ISIS are getting better at building IEDs, and last year, they had over one thousand successful bomb attacks. If we called for them, how many dogs could you get me?"

"Oh no. Not me. I don't train combat animals. These ones are just for detection or search and rescue. I won't put any of mine in the line of fire."

Rich continued, "General, you need solid military working dogs that can keep up with the Special Forces deployed in Afghanistan. This requires a special breed—ones that can be trained in all MWD disciplines. I think you've heard of that facility in northeast Texas that is developing these animals. I know the guy running it. He's former Special Forces and has some well qualified trainers on his staff. I think you'll find what you're looking for there."

###

At that non-descript clapboard-covered breeding and training facility Rich described, he came into the world, destined to become the best one percent of the best one percent. The last of a litter of five, he was a bit smaller than his brothers and sisters. Half German Shepherd and half Belgian Malinois, he had black ears and a bushier tail than most of the others in the kennel. Unlike most German Shepherds, his hindquarters were proportional to his front, enabling him to have a long, smooth and even stride. Down his back ran a line of black fur that zigzagged through the tan from his neck to the base of his tail.

The family stayed together for six weeks until it was time for the pups to be weaned away from their mother. Master Sergeant Manny Blanco watched the litter interact for hours on end, noting the differences between each of the pups. He noted how they played, how they reacted to sound, if they startled easily, or quickly gave up when playing tug of war or wrestling. The sergeant had a trained eye for what made a dog special.

He was looking for the ones that had the unique qualities needed to become Special Forces K9 service dogs. As he dictated his thoughts into the memo function of his iPhone, he found himself making more notes about the small one than any of the others. The diminutive fuzzy one had an awareness about him that was well beyond the others'.

When a playful dogfight broke out, the pup with the black

zigzag could size up his brothers and sisters instantly, and knew when to charge in and when to back off. His positional awareness was special. He could assess a situation quickly to determine if he had the advantage for reaching a toy or treat before anyone else. When he was out of position, he could distract the others with a sudden movement, giving him the fraction of a second he needed to make his move. Above all, however, the dog knew people.

He was aware of them. While the others never paid much attention to Manny as he made his observations, the small one noticed. He would look at Manny and lock eyes, not to challenge—which is the nature of most dogs—but as if to collect information and make a connection. Manny became fascinated with the small one and started to call him Zip because of his quickness and the way he darted back and forth around the kennel. It wasn't the toughest sounding name, but it fit.

"What do you think?" Manny said to his partner, Chloe Van Raalten, as he motioned his head towards Zip.

"What, the little one?" Chloe responded, a bit surprised.

"Yeah, take a look at him. He always out-maneuvers the other dogs and has an uncanny awareness. See, he's looking at us now, like he knows we're talking about him."

"I don't like the smart ones," she replied dismissively, and in a completely business-like manner as she began to rattle off Zip's negatives. "We need doers, not thinkers. Dogs with a mind of their own tend to do what they want, not what we want. Most of them are cowards. They know better than to put themselves in harm's way. Anyway, I don't like the mixed breeds. You know that. Purebred Belgian Malinois are better suited to our needs. This one's got too much shepherd in him. He's going to get hip dysplasia, just you wait. Plus, he's cute. I don't do cute."

"True, maybe," Manny replied. "But watch him. He's a born worker. Since he was able to walk, he moves around always looking for something to do. He may look like a shepherd but he's got the heart of a Malinois. And I think he'll stay small, which is a plus for when he has to be carried or tethered for fast roping from the choppers."

Zip was drawn to the sound of their conversation. He took a seat about ten feet away from the two and listened to the tones of their voices and their speech patterns. The mane of fur surrounding his face made him look just like a German Shepherd and the way his triangular ears moved was like twitching antennae as he tried to process their words into useable information. Those ears conveyed emotion and intelligence.

Finally Chloe capitulated, "Look, if you want to waste a quarter of a million dollars of government money to train and equip the mutt, that's your call. You're the boss. But I don't think he's the right candidate for Special Forces."

"Well, I'll get him out in the next couple weeks and see how he does, but I'll want you to work with him a while, too."

Manny Blanco was in a unique position. He retained his old Army rank, even though he was no longer on active duty. He was a reservist, but he was working on a very particular project for the U.S. Special Forces and Navy in particular. Manny had spent the past two years establishing a special school to breed and train military working dogs, typically referred to by the acronym "MWD." Up to this point, most military units traveled to Europe to identify and buy their working dogs, as did law enforcement agencies. They usually had initial training done in Holland, Belgium, or the Czech or Slovakian Republics. As the value of MWDs continued to appreciate, the U.S. Military decided it might be worthwhile to establish a stronger domestic breeding and training program.

Manny was a pioneer in this area. He had spent most of his adult life in the military, having joined the Army right out of high school, and practically all of it working with these fine animals. His first contact with MWDs was as a young MP, where he began to realize their value. Later, as an Army Ranger, he witnessed their effectiveness in both unconventional and direct combat missions. Where he perfected his skills, however, was as a member of the elite Navy SEALs, following a rare branch transfer. Few had seen special ops from his vantage point. Manny served in the first Gulf War, Somalia, and an initial tour in Iraq following 9/11. Throughout each tour, he came to know courageous K9 troops, developing an affinity for them as well as a reputation as one of the best military dog handlers in the world.

After Iraq, he was transferred back to the states where he finished out his active duty helping to select and train MWDs. He became the foremost authority on identifying the qualities of the best working dogs. Now, he was tasked with managing the domestic program through his privately owned school, which had an exclusive contract with the U.S. Special Forces.

As soon as Manny thought Zip was ready, he took him out to run him through the paces. First, he exposed Zip to the sounds of combat. Dogs that showed anxiety around loud noises such as thunder, gunfire, or explosions were automatically considered unfit for special duty. As he worked alongside Manny, Zip grew accustomed to the sounds. And while Manny could tell the noise sometimes hurt his ears, the dog never broke stride or cowered while on parade. It was a good start.

Next, he needed to see how Zip would respond to commands. Manny practiced him vigorously on trigger words designed to instill discipline, including commands calling on and off attack, and special words and hand motions to signal quiet, or to drop and stay low. Zip could sometimes be obstinate when he grew tired of the lessons. Then he would simply shut down, taking a comfortable spot in the grass and turning his back to Manny. More than once during the early part of his training Zip was nearly washed out of the program. In time, though, Zip became more and more responsive. Manny finally felt they were at the point where Chloe could make some progress with him.

Chloe and Manny were strictly business partners. He had hired her away from one of the elite K9 schools in the Netherlands. Chloe was gifted with an amazing patience for animals, and worked with them extensively on the routine tasks, such as learning commands, which she taught Zip to recognize in both English and Dutch. They went over and over basic disciplined maneuvers. She got him used to walking over strange or different surfaces like rocks and open grates without hesitation.

Chloe trained Zip to navigate all sorts of hazards and to think three dimensionally so he could scale near-vertical ladders and walk on narrow balance beams without fear or hesitation. Before long, Zip accomplished the K9 obstacle course in record time. As she spent long hours working with him, she realized that Zip was no ordinary dog and her initial assessment had been premature.

After he mastered commands and maneuvers, Zip and Chloe worked to perfect his seeking and detection abilities by engaging in increasingly complex drills. At first, she arranged boxes that contained different scents. The object was to identify the one that held the "target" scent. When Zip was told to search, or "zoek" in Dutch, Chloe was always amazed at how Zip hesitated momentarily before beginning the search. He always paused and looked at her, as if trying to determine a "tell" that might tip him off to where the target box was. Most working dogs began a search almost franticly with nose to the ground, quickly moving back and forth and around the items they are directed to examine. But not Zip. He was more methodical. He moved with surprising efficiency when looking for the target. When he was sure he had found the specified item, he would either become rigid and identify the object by pointing, or just sit down and look back at Chloe as if to say, "That's all you got?" As they worked to hone his skills, Zip became adept at identifying over a hundred different scents including the chemical compounds used in various types of explosives. He could distinguish between those commonly used in U.S. manufactured weapons and those developed by adversaries.

Finally, she taught him how to track and pursue. Zip's sense of smell was not nearly as developed as a bloodhound's, and so he had to learn the process of ground disturbance tracking. While bloodhounds can detect smells in the air left by the person being trailed, Zip could not and had to keep his nose close to the ground where footsteps disturbed surrounding soil and the human tang was most concentrated. Scents were more difficult to detect dependent on the hardness of the surface. However, Zip did well and could follow any number of scents over great distances without losing the trail. Once he was on to the smell of his prey, there was no escape.

Play was his reward for a hard day's work. After Zip completed hours of training, he looked forward to his down time. This was the period when he could play tug-of-war or chase a ball with Manny, or just spend some quality time chewing up a rawhide. Zip's favorite activity was catching a Frisbee. When he finished all his lessons, Manny would move towards Zip's footlocker, which contained his various training aides and toys. Zip's ears pointed straight up and he tilted his head to one side, waiting and watching for that battered red disc to come out of his box. When it did, Zip would spin around and dart for the door like a bolt of lightning, reinforcing his metaphoric name.

Manny could whip that disc a full seventy-five yards, and Zip could chase it down so fast that he was able to leap into the air and snag the toy from the sky while it was still more than six feet off the ground. As Zip chased after the Frisbee, he pinned his ears to the side of his head and used his tail like a rudder to cut through the air, making turns on a dime. When it was time to leap, he pushed off with his strong hind legs that flared out to the sides, as if he had wings. He clamped down on the Frisbee and dropped elegantly to the ground, spinning around before heading back to Manny with his head high in a deliberate, almost cocky, trot. Manny sometimes had to drag Zip off the field when it was time to quit.

SEAL stands for Sea, Air and Land. A Navy SEAL must master each of these environments. Dogs chosen to become part of these elite teams are no different. When the order came in for a SEAL K9, Manny knew Zip was the one. His land-based skills were already best in class. But they still had a lot more work to do.

Chapter 2
Forged by Adversity

As it was for his human counterparts, there would be grueling training to learn how to survive in the elements and, like human SEAL candidates, most dogs were broken by the stress and rejected from the program. If a dog panicked under fire or during a maneuver, it could mean death for both dog and partner. Manny had to be certain that Zip could handle any type of stressful environment.

Water. That would be the first test. They drove the short distance to the reservoir and Manny led Zip onto the waiting boat. The captain took it out a full half-mile off shore, until there was no land was in sight. Manny needed to gauge how well Zip could handle the stress of being thrown in the water with no land as a frame of reference. Would he panic and flail wildly towards Manny in order to be saved, or would he remain calm and trust in Manny's commands to get them safely back to shore? Manny went over the side first—the water in Jim Chapman Lake was cold, as it always was in early spring. Then Chloe lowered Zip. He was equipped with a canine buoyancy vest, in case he panicked or became exhausted on the swim back to shore. The boat pulled away leaving

Zip and Manny alone in the water. The moment was crucial. Manny had to know how Zip would react to the fact that their only dry platform was gone. Zip paddled in place as he watched the boat slip into the distance, and listened intently to the sound of the engines fading away. Then there was silence. Manny tread water slowly, remaining still to see how Zip would react to the water, the calmness, and the complete absence of reference points.

Zip looked at Manny and let out a whimper but made no move as if to panic. Manny let a full five minutes go by. Zip simply paddled in a circle as if trying to figure out which way to go. Finally, Manny gave a command and began swimming in the direction they had come from in the boat. Zip dutifully followed. He didn't especially like the water. It got in his ears and nose, making it difficult to concentrate and maintain full awareness of his surroundings. However, he had grown to trust his handler and knew that Manny had never yet let harm come to him. Zip had no reason to believe he would today. As they swam together towards shore, Zip became more comfortable and assured they were going towards safety. He could smell the pines and crape myrtles—that meant land was near. Manny's strong, rhythmic swimming strokes calmed him, too. He could handle the sea—he was going to be fine.

The air was his next test. Manny knew that these highly specialized animals had to get used to riding in all types of military vehicles, and that they particularly had to be comfortable with helicopters. Since the training facility was near an Army Reserve Center, Zip had already seen helicopters—lots of them. He even learned to recognize the different ones coming and going just by the sound of their rotors. But he had not yet ridden in one.

Manny also knew that exceptional dogs could handle almost every other aspect of their training, but if they washed out of the program it almost always had to do with the anxiety of flying. Even more than simply being comfortable with flying, Manny had to prepare Zip to jump out of aircraft.

They started by walking around the hangars and the tarmac. Zip sniffed around the helicopters at rest, picking up all the normal odors from fuel, hot metal, the occasional bit of fresh paint or putty—and of course the scent left behind by the people touching the choppers as they boarded or worked on the engines. Manny let him put his paws up on the low doorways and peer inside. More smells of canvas, leather, weapons, boots. Not so bad. It looked a little like the inside of Manny's truck. The next time Manny took him to the airfield, they walked around a chopper with the engines and rotors engaged. The motor noises didn't bother him so much. After all, they had worked on that a lot. But the whump, whump, whump and wind of the rotor wash took a little getting used to. Finally, the big day came and Manny boarded Zip onto the helicopter for a short ride, followed by another and another. Zip adapted slowly but not without a bit of angst. Flying would never be his favorite exercise.

Later, Manny fitted Zip with a special harness. Zip practiced being lifted up off the ground, just a few feet at a time. The sensation of feeling no grass or concrete or carpet under his paws, no weight on his legs, was disorienting at first. Zip didn't get the point. And just when he started to get used to hanging there, Manny gave the harness a nudge and he began to gently swing, back and forth. This was completely alien to Zip and he couldn't understand why Manny was making him flounder around in the air. Everything in his training so far had been in line with furthering the development of aspects of his own canine drives. The swimming and hunting, smelling out objects, fighting and playing—even all the endless commands—had meaning, either restraining him from or pushing him toward the pursuit of his own proclivities. But this experience, this bird stuff, this was entirely alien. Why was Manny pulling him off the ground, higher and higher, and then swinging him back and forth? Zip didn't like it, and not only because it made him uncomfortable. It had no real purpose. But he accepted it.

Manny now felt that, after all his extensive efforts at adaptation, Zip was ready for the next step in his transformation towards becoming a highly disciplined asset with all the skills necessary for the U.S. Special Forces. He fitted Zip in a new vest with buckles and hooks on it. It was time to suit up.

Zip rather liked it, and the slight clinking noise it made when he shook himself. He held himself as though he was proud of his new vest. But then Manny put things over his eyes. Zip hated the "doggles." He could deal with the vests and paw covers and all the other stuff they strapped to him, but he could not stand to have anything covering his face and eyes. It took him a long time to get used to the glasses. In the end, he simply tolerated them, tugging them from his eyes with his paw at the first opportunity.

Finally, in the first minutes of daylight on what promised to be a very hot summer morning, the time for reckoning arrived. Dog, trainer, pilots, and attendants loaded into the helicopter and lifted from the ground. Zip's stomach dropped and his ears began to hurt as they pulled higher into the air. Chopper rides were not like the harness training just feet or yards off the ground. He went up and up, further from the land, like when he was in the lake, only worse. The sides of the helicopter were open and Zip made sure to stay firmly planted in the middle of the cabin, as he had during his other rides. The air and the sound rushed together and there was so much wind, it took all the smell away. This was always when he felt the most helpless.

The helicopter had moved out above the forest and Zip could see the trees in the distance when Manny gave a command, "Zip, come!" But he was crouched by the edge of the door, dangerously close to falling out and way too close for an intelligent dog to do any "coming." Zip didn't budge. Then Manny repeated, in a sterner tone, "Zip, come!"

Torn by his drive for self-preservation and his near-automatic response to obey commands, Zip started to move forward, haltingly, with his tail tight between his legs and ears pasted to his head. His back was hunched and his movements were agonizingly slow. He would "come" alright, but he wasn't going to be in any hurry to get there. As he inched closer, he felt Manny grab hold of the harness and clip him to two ropes hanging above him from the bulkhead. The helicopter slowed down and stayed in one place in the air. They had hovered before. But something didn't feel right.

Suddenly, Manny acted in a way that that Zip just could not believe—he pushed him out over the edge of the doorway! The harness and rope jerked tight against his chest, and he didn't fall. But he was just hanging there, suspended in the breeze, under the helicopter—alone! The sounds and the space were too much. Zip pawed frantically, desperate to make traction and somehow get back up to the helicopter. Why would Manny do this! Why was he out here all alone? Then the helicopter tilted slightly, transitioning to forward flight. Zip yelped and drove his legs as if galloping in mid-air. It was no use; he had no control over the situation. He was helpless and afraid, and he closed his eyes.

Then, he felt a presence and could smell Manny. Zip opened his eyes to see Manny hanging with him, right beside him. Zip lunged as Manny grabbed his harness and pulled him in tight to his body. They were still moving forward high above the trees, but Manny had a strong grip on him. Zip buried his head in Manny's chest and, after a few moments, began to calm himself. They were together, dog and partner. He was safe.

There were more rides and more jumps. As time went on, Zip got more used to the exercise and even the idea of being suspended from a helicopter. He learned how to stay close to his trainers during those unsettling times, gaining confidence that the actions of his trainers would not intentionally put him in danger. It was the painstaking ritual of trust building that moved Zip over the goal line in his transformation from useful domesticated animal to a valuable team member of the United States Special Forces.

When Manny and Chloe were one hundred percent satisfied that Zip had learned the essentials that Special Forces required, Manny tattooed Zip's unique military working dog identification number on the inside flesh of one ear. In the other, he tattooed the trident symbol of the U.S. Navy SEALs.

Chapter 3
He Stands Alongside America's Finest Special Operations Forces

Manny knew he was only the first rung on Zip's ladder. He understood that his role was to identify, condition, and train dogs for their future roles in the military. It was his job to determine where they were best fit for duty, and he was exceedingly adept at it. When Manny and Zip had been together for a full year, Manny readied himself for the time to come when he would have to turn Zip over to the people who would become his partners and unit. He had trained hundreds of dogs and the separating never got easier. But saying goodbye this time would be tough.

Manny, Chloe, and Zip spent hundreds of hours together and, because of that, Zip was now highly trained and proficient. He was supremely disciplined for his duty. He could swim for great distances and remain calm in any type of aircraft. He could detect the smell of a wide variety of explosives and identify them for his partner. He was tough. He could attack on command in the blink of an eye and withdraw in the same moment. Above all, Zip was smart. The smartest Manny had ever trained. The dog had situational awareness, which was exceedingly rare. For an animal, even one trained to react to commands, to sometimes forego his own animal impulses depending on circumstance was unusual. Zip seemed to have a unique intuition for people. He could distinguish those who were genuine from those operating under false pretenses simply by the tone of their voice or demeanor. Manny was certain he would be an exceptional SEAL.

Manny took great measures to not get too close to any of his dogs. There was no association outside of training or "reward play." Zip had slept in the kennel with the other dogs, away from off-duty contact with his humans. Manny tried to keep it all business, like he did with the other K9s.

Zip liked Manny. He had come to trust him, and he was the only "Dad" he knew. Although there were other people around throughout his training, there was no one he was closer to than Manny, except maybe Chloe. But she wasn't the one Zip looked forward to seeing. There was no way Zip could understand he was about to leave and they would probably never see each other again. There was just something in Manny's voice that gave him the impression that things were about to change.

Naval Amphibious Base, Little Creek, in Virginia is one of two main training headquarters for the U.S. Navy SEALs. It administers the toughest training regimen in any military. So far as Manny was concerned, those who graduated from the Basic Underwater Demolition/SEAL or BUD/S program were the best combat troops in the world. Zip would fit right in.

Manny pulled the Humvee up to the series of barracks that served as the current training housing for the platoons that made up SEAL Team 4. This was a tough bunch of men who had been together through a deployment in Iraq and two more in Afghanistan. The barracks that Manny parked beside quartered the first squad of the second platoon. Petty Officer First Class Ted "Boomer" Stock heard the vehicle pull up and, opening the screen door, was the first to see Manny unloading a dog from the back of the truck.

"Hey Mitchell, your new fuzzy boyfriend's here," Stock bellowed over his shoulder and through the barracks. As he stepped out the door toward Manny, Zip hit the blacktop.

Automatically, Zip sized up Stock, and Stock did the same.

"Kind of small, isn't he? Why do you need such a big vehicle for such a little dog?" he said half-jokingly.

"He'll get the job done," Manny shot back without cracking a smile in response to the first question while ignoring the second.

Zip took a longer look at the SEAL and let his scent register. He was big—well over six feet—with broad shoulders and a shaved head that glimmered when the sun hit it. And he smelled like pickles. Zip stared at him some more. He sensed a gentle spirit.

Petty Officer First Class Todd Mitchell stepped out of the barracks to meet the new teammate. He was trained specially as a handler and had leaped at the chance for a K9 partner.

When command had decided that most SEAL Teams would be assigned at least one K9 in the units, Todd had already been a SEAL for three years. The success of the raid on Osama bin Laden and the involvement of a K9 SEAL named Cairo cemented the reputation these dogs had for considerable abilities. It was a public relations boon for the SEALs.

Historically, most of the K9 handlers were not SEALs themselves. They were MWD specialists assigned to each SEAL Team. In more recent times, the direct role of dogs working with the SEAL Teams and their handlers had evolved. Whereas Manny's team were specialists at developing dogs specifically bound for the Special Forces, the expanded K9 program was a bit different for U.S. Navy SEALs, who were always on the cutting edge of military tactics and innovation. Todd had volunteered to get in on the ground floor.

Manny walked up to Mitchell and handed him Zip's lead. "OK, let's take him out and let him get used to you."

Todd took the lead, and then he paused and dropped to a knee. He and Zip stared at each other for a long minute. Todd wanted to make a good first impression on Zip. He wanted him to know that he did not intend to be a "master," and demonstrated it by lowering himself to Zip's level. Todd wanted a partner, someone who could operate efficiently with the brothers of his SEAL Team.

Dogs have an extra sense beyond sight, smell, hearing, touch, and taste. It allows them, sometimes, to make a near-instant judgment about and connection with certain humans. Zip sensed it with this particular man. He was different than Manny or Chloe, and Zip wanted to learn more about him.

For the next two hours, Todd and Manny worked together with

Zip on transferring the basic commands and getting him accustomed to taking orders from a different partner. Often, during these transfers, it could take a while for the animal to get it. But Manny was surprised at the synchronicity these two developed almost instantly. He wasn't sure if he felt pleased with Zip's skills, or just the slightest twinge of jealously.

When they finished, the three walked back to the barracks where Todd nonchalantly opened the door and motioned Zip inside with an "In you go, Boy."

"Hey," Manny said, stopping him. "You don't intend to let him stay in the barracks with you–do you?"

"Why sure, Master Sergeant. Why not?"

"Because that's against every regulation."

"Oh, well, that's not going to be a problem," Todd said.

"And why is that?"

"Because we're not going to tell anyone."

Before they walked into the barracks, Manny stopped them one more time "I'm telling you Petty Officer, this one's special. Take care of him and he will do the same for you."

He handed Todd a small bag of toys and turned back to the Humvee. "He likes to catch Frisbee," Manny said over his shoulder as he made it to the driver's side door. He paused, hand on handle, looked back at Zip and shouted, "They're all yours now, Boy."

Zip trotted over to Manny and sat at his feet, looking only slightly irritated. Manny bent down and scratched Zip under the chin one last time, then hopped in the Humvee and drove off without another word. Zip trotted back to Todd.

Boomer was leaning against the barracks doorway as they approached.

"What the hell kind of a name is 'Zip'?" he said dryly as the sound of the Humvee faded in the distance.

"What the hell kind of a name is Boomer?" Todd retorted. "Maybe we should call the *dog* Boomer."

"Sorry, that's taken. He probably couldn't live up to it."

The two friends chuckled and walked Zip into the barracks, holding the screen door ceremoniously for their new teammate.

The barracks was clean, remarkably clean. Zip had never spent any real time in a building that had people in it, and he certainly never slept in the same quarters with them. It appeared that these particular SEALs were going to consider him a full member of their team. They told him they expected the same discipline and order from him that they would from any other SEAL. After all, when it came time to deploy in a combat situation, he would be sleeping with them, and so in their minds he should do the same stateside. It took Zip a second for his eyes to adjust but the smells hit him instantly. There was the cleaner with that chemical scent that burned his nose. They must use a lot of it here. The smells of aftershave, chewing tobacco, dirty socks, clean socks—it was an assault on his nose. Oh, and pickles. But it was the unique smell of each man in the unit that excited him. Zip wanted to know everything about these humans. He knew Todd was to be his handler, but he didn't know yet that they would become best friends.

Todd Mitchell grew up in the hills outside of Pittsburgh. An all-state hockey player, he went to Penn State on an athletic scholarship for two years before deciding to drop out and join the Navy. He'd always had a hard head and just couldn't muster the academic focus he needed to complete a degree. That decision made for a big falling out with his dad. The elder Mitchell had visions of his son joining his successful law practice; maybe even taking over the business one day. It was Bob Mitchell's dream, not Todd's, and he just couldn't live up to his father's expectations anymore.

Todd married Lindsey, his high school sweetheart, right after he earned his trident. Now, they had a baby on the way. He loved the Navy as much as he loved his new family and felt an equal commitment to both.

Boomer Stock was the comedian of the outfit and the perfect foil for Todd's headstrong, serious manner. He was also his closest friend. The man had the ability to find humor in anything and everything, even when the team found itself in extreme situations. It was his attitude that kept the team going during several desperate engagements. He, too, started a college career on an athletic scholarship (at Georgia Tech). But when a knee injury ended his football career, he ended his college career and joined the Navy. Boomer had a propensity to drink pickle juice as part of his workout routine. He was convinced that the amino acids in the juice gave him an advantage during workouts and allowed for faster muscle recovery time. Zip liked him and felt comfortable in his presence.

Senior Chief Petty Officer R.J. Robbins was their Communications Specialist and the highest ranking member of the squad. He was a supreme technophile from Seattle who had an amazing ability to fix nearly anything electrical by piecing together any components he could scrounge. A self-taught programmer and avid radio control airplane nut, he was a study in perpetual motion. When he wasn't tinkering with the equipment, he was working out. He had developed a number of eponymous CrossFit routines that were nearly impossible to complete and was still trying to outdo himself. R.J. never wasted a minute.

One of the most valuable members of any SEAL Team is the Navy Corpsman. Trained as a SEAL and specializing in trauma medicine, Eric "Old Doc" Burkich was the team's curmudgeon. Old Doc was so tagged by the team because he was mature beyond his twenty-five years. When Todd and Zip walked into the barracks, he was deep into a manual on emergency veterinary canine care. If there was a new member on the team, Old Doc Burk was going to make sure he knew how to treat him. He always had a dip of Copenhagen in his lower lip.

Petty Officer First Class Jeff "Angel" Nakamura sat on the edge of his bunk and eyed the new team member as he entered. He was the team's sniper and heavy weapons specialist. He was slim and incredibly adroit at concealment. If he didn't want to be seen, no one was going to find him. Each member of the team felt an added sense of security knowing that Angel Nakamura watched over them from some unseen location.

The balance of the eight-man squad comprised three more exceptional SEALs. Petty Officer Third Class Michael "Radar" Hancock was the Technical Surveillance Specialist. Petty Officer Second Class Scott Penman was the linguistics and interrogation specialist who possessed such a remarkable ability to pick out voices and accents that he could do spot on impressions of everyone in the platoon. Lastly, Petty Officer Third Class Jim Fox was the team's Point Man/Navigator, and the youngest member of the team at just twenty years old.

Zip paced the length of the barracks deliberately, approaching each member of his new team and memorizing their distinctive scents. He then walked over to Todd at his bunk and took a glance at the small dog bed near the foot of the bunk. Zip decided that it was not up to his standards and promptly leaped onto Todd's rack, sprawling out and making himself right at home.

"Hey!" Todd yelled.

Zip nudged the pillow off the bunk and rolled over to his back.

"Well-trained, isn't he?" Boomer said as the rest of the team laughed.

"You know, he does outrank you," Old Doc Burk offered from across the room. "So maybe he deserves the bunk."

"What's that?" Fox sounded confused.

"Yep," Old Doc said. "All military working dogs obtain a rank one grade higher than the handler. That way, the handler can easily be brought up on charges if there's any sign of abuse."

Just about then, the door burst opened and a strong tenor voice put an abrupt end to the levity.

"Petty Officer Mitchell! What is that animal doing on your rack?"

The distinctive voice belonged to Lieutenant John Kelly, platoon commander. Kelly was a Naval Academy graduate and hard core all the way. The team knew him well. Not unlike Zip, he possessed a unique situational awareness and a sixth sense for danger. His tactical awareness was uncanny. He signed up for the SEALs the day after graduating from the Academy and dedicated his life to the Special Forces. Everyone in the squad had the utmost respect for Lieutenant Kelly. They all knew he had the team's back if all hell broke loose. Kelly was a devout Roman Catholic who visited the base chapel every day, or took time to pray the rosary when in the field. At only five feet eight inches, he was compact. But he cut an imposing figure and, with only eight percent body fat, he was the best swimmer in all of SEAL Team 4.

Zip's head popped up, too, at the sound of his voice. His ears pinned back against his head and he jumped down from Todd's bunk to curl up on his own little bed. Zip understood right away that this was a man not to be tested.

That first night in the barracks, Zip lay quietly on his bed listening to the sounds of the conversations of the men in the squad. He loved the tones of their voices as they joked at each other's expense. No one was spared from the good-natured banter. He was getting a sense of their loyalty to each other and was happy to be in their presence. For the first time, he felt like he was part of a pack, and he knew it was good.

Discipline, commitment, and loyalty are the primary tenets of any SEAL Team. Zip had learned the structure for all of this during his time with Manny. Now it was time to become fully integrated into his new family.

Chapter 4
My Training is Never Complete

Training and more training—SEALs thrive on it and Lieutenant Kelly was going to ensure that his platoon would not jeopardize any operation, particularly as the first squad on base with a new four-legged team member. He was leery of having an animal in his platoon, even though he'd researched their effectiveness. He had to be sure he could trust everyone on his team, including and especially a K9.

The team's day routinely started at 0600. Of course, R.J. led the pack by being up and into his own workout by 0500. He liked to set the standard for the team to follow, and as he rose from his bunk the morning after Zip arrived, he peered through the darkness over to Zip's bed to see if the new guy was up. Two glowing eyes stared back at him. They looked at each other for a moment as R.J. pulled on his shorts. When he headed for the door, Zip rose from his bed, walked over to tell R.J. good morning, then turned around and headed back to his bunk.

"Not ready for me yet, eh Boy?" R.J. said as he jogged out the door.

The rest of the team rose at 0600 and headed out for morning

PT before chow. Zip did the five miles with the team and sat at attention while they worked through calisthenics. When they finished, the entire squad headed for the base galley. Zip was at Todd's side as they walked into the hall. A Petty Officer stopped them at the door.

"Just what do you think you're doing?' he barked.

"We're going to chow," Todd replied evenly.

"Not with that you're not," The Petty Officer said, glaring at Zip.

"THAT," Todd said with and edge to his voice, "is a U.S. Navy SEAL assigned to the First Squad, Second Platoon of SEAL Team 4. Where we go, he goes."

With that he pushed by, Zip in tow, determined to make his point. The Petty Officer knew better than to challenge him, instead retreating to the rear of the galley. He would just send this matter up the chain, and went to the grab the Master Chief in charge of the hall.

Master Chief Sullivan emerged from his makeshift office, wiping perspiration from his neck with a dish towel.

"Petty Officer!" the Master Chief bellowed as he marched toward them. "Where do you get off breaking regulations by bringing that animal into my galley?"

By now, the rest of the squad had filed in and noticed that a situation was starting to develop. They all knew that Todd was not going to back down from this. He didn't like to be challenged, especially by some "cookie."

Just then Boomer piped up, "Can't you see Master Chief? This is a new experimental gilly suit. This is actually Seaman Zipster. Had you fooled, didn't he?"

Sullivan wasn't in the mood this morning and he didn't like being played for a fool by a bunch of smart-ass elitists.

"Get him out!"

No one moved. Todd was in the wrong and knew that he couldn't possibly win. But he didn't care.

As the standoff continued and Todd inched closer and closer to landing himself into a severe disciplinary situation, Lieutenant Kelly appeared from nowhere.

"What the hell is going on in here?" Kelly asked. He was stern, but remarkably calm.

"Sir," Sullivan said with very little respect in his voice, "This situation is a clear breach of Navy regs. I have worked with these animals before and they are never allowed in the galley. Your Petty Officer here knows it but seems to have his own ideas about how the Navy works."

"Lieutenant," Todd began, "everything about this is irregular. This is a relatively new program and we need to have these dogs close to us at all times. I have been assigned to develop this one and I need to see what he is capable of and where and if he might break. I can't make a proper assessment of his capabilities and limitations if I'm continually forced to comply with these 'regulations of convenience', Sir."

Lieutenant Kelly took Sullivan aside. "Master Chief, I know this is not in keeping with normal Navy regulations and I know you are aware of our unique assignments. You are welcome to communicate this through channels and I encourage you to make a proper report. However, at this time, I intend to keep my team together so that they become the well-oiled machine I expect them to be."

"Very well, Lieutenant. It's your ass. Don't expect me to cover for your boys. Anyway, I don't have food here for him. We were never informed."

"Understood Master Chief," Kelly said, abruptly spinning away. Then he approached Todd and Zip.

"Look Mitchell, I am sticking my neck out for you here and I really don't appreciate this self-righteous defiance that's already made you infamous on this base. You're not doing yourself or that dog any favors by always trying to buck the system. Now, there's no food here for him so I want you to get him something to hold him over for today. Get off the base tonight and get him enough food to last until we can get it properly requisitioned."

"Yes Sir," Todd said quietly.

"Take the squad and go to the aft table on the port side—and no more incidents."

Todd took Zip back as ordered and found him a bowlful of eggs, sausage, and rice with an additional bowl of water. He made sure Zip stayed in place while they and the rest of the squad ate quickly, then quietly made their way out of the galley.

John Kelly knew how to work a system and thereafter Todd was able to take Zip into the dining facility without further incident. Whatever regulation they were violating was tacitly ignored, much to Master Chief Sullivan's chagrin.

The balance of the day was spent drilling urban warfare and the sweeping and clearing of buildings. Lieutenant Kelly wanted to see how Zip interacted with the team and how he followed orders. He was surprised at how efficient Zip was, having had no experience working with any of these people before. Zip held his position as doors were wired and blown off their hinges. When a flash bang grenade was thrown into a space, he knew not to chase after it. He had been trained to lower his head and turn it aside when such a device was thrown into a room, and then wait for the command to enter. When entering a room, he immediately responded to orders to search for people, weapons, or explosives. The team repeated these entries for the rest of the afternoon until Kelly was comfortable that their performance was replicable and that Zip had the discipline necessary for the task.

The team finished drilling at 1600 and cleaned up their gear. Boomer, Todd, and Zip went off base for a quick dog chow run, picking up the food Kelly had specified. When they returned to base, there was still quite a bit of daylight left.

"Hey Boomer!" Todd yelled. "Let's take Zip over to Tarralton Park and see what he can do with the Frisbee before the sun goes down."

Todd grabbed the red disc and as soon as Zip caught sight of it, he was up with eyes focused and ears at attention. The three jumped into Todd's Jeep Wrangler and Zip instantly commandeered the front passenger seat.

"Not gonna happen, Fuzz Butt," Boomer said and pushed him off the seat.

Zip moved off and to the back, but not without first shooting Boomer what could only be described as a glare of indignation.

"Hey! He's a pretentious A-Hole, just like you," Boomer joked as they drove off to the park. "You two are going to get along great!"

Tarralton Park was just on the edge of the base and had a series of baseball fields with a large open area in the middle. There were some others milling around, enjoying the park, and a few people were walking their dogs. But Zip took little notice of anything but the Frisbee under Todd's arm. They walked to the edge of the field and Todd took Zip off his lead. Zip spun in front of him in excitement, then stopped and stared intently at the Frisbee. Todd snapped his wrist and the disc sailed in the calmness of the early evening air. Zip whipped himself around and was off after the disc like a rocket. Todd made a good throw and the Frisbee floated about ten feet off the ground.

"Holy Cow, look at him go!" Boomer exclaimed.

Zip kept his eyes on the Frisbee the entire time it was aloft. When he bolted from Todd's feet, the disc was about twenty yards ahead of him, but he quickly closed the distance in a few strides. As the Frisbee slowed down and started to drift towards the ground, Zip didn't wait for it to land. He pulled his front paws into his chest and pushed off with his strong back legs, snatching it from the air.

"Man, can he fly!" Todd said.

"For sure! You guys can have another career doing halftime shows when you get out."

The three spent the rest of the available daylight chasing the Frisbee and when they couldn't see it against the sky anymore they headed directly back to the barracks. Zip was spent. He slurped down a full bowl of water and jumped into Todd's bunk for his night's rest. Todd let him go and gave him a pat. Then he and the team went to the Time Out Sports Bar for some wings, a couple of beers, and to review the day. Todd wanted to hear what they thought of Zip's performance. To a man, the feedback was positive. Each of them was impressed with how quickly Zip had assimilated. When they got back to the barracks, Todd shooed Zip off his rack and took him out one last time.

"You did OK, Boy. You did real well," Todd said as they walked in the dark. And the squad called it a day.

SEAL training can last weeks or months. On the weekends, the team split up and went to their own off-base housing. Todd and Lindsey had kept a small one-bedroom apartment not far from base, but as her pregnancy progressed they decided that Lindsey would go back home to Pittsburgh to be near both of their families. Right before Zip had arrived, Lindsey moved to her grandparents' place. They owned and operated a small dairy farm just outside Burgettstown, PA. There was an additional small house on the farm and they were close to an excellent network of hospitals in the area. Todd felt better having her near family. But this meant Zip and Todd had to "batch" it on the weekends. They would go back to the apartment, where Zip made himself right at home. No piece of furniture was off limits, no matter how hard Todd tried. Todd was baffled by how disciplined this dog could be when it was time to work, but what an obstinate slob he was off duty.

The training regimen went on for another month. Lieutenant Kelly kept pushing the limits to integrate Zip into the unit. He worked out complex drills to see how Zip and the team would adjust. When checking for improvised explosive devices, or IEDs, Kelly would place secondary devices and trip wires on the path to see if Zip could detect them and to ensure he wouldn't inadvertently detonate a bomb. He mixed up the types of explosives to see if he could detect the differences. Later, they put Zip in the air to see how he could handle the fast rope.

In every drill, Zip appeared to adapt and in so doing, prove his worth. Sometimes, Lieutenant Kelly thought that Todd might be cheating the system and giving Zip clues or otherwise tipping him off. Slowly, Kelly started to entertain the possibility that Zip really was that good.

Near the end of the month, the team was scheduled to do a HALO jump. HALO stands for High Altitude, Low Opening. The SEALs would jump with parachutes from an altitude so high that oxygen was required, often from greater than twenty thousand feet, then freefall until opening the chute at an altitude of less than a thousand feet. The team was hesitant to let Todd and Zip make this kind of jump. There were few SEALs who had ever done it with a dog strapped to their stomach, and it was a dangerous maneuver under the best of circumstances. Two days before the jump, Todd spent time getting Zip used to the K9 oxygen mask he would have to wear. They worked on having Zip strapped to him and still being able to reach his ripcord and secondary cord. Zip had to wear the hated "doggles" and continued to push them off every chance he had.

On the day of the jump, Lieutenant Kelly was still hesitant about letting the team go up with a dog, but Todd assured him that both he and Zip were ready. The team loaded into the adapted C160 Cargo aircraft for the jump and Zip trotted up the ramp by Todd's side. As the plane lifted off, Zip felt that now familiar pain in his ears but soon acclimated to the altitude. The aircraft lifted higher above the clouds and the team was given the indication to go on oxygen. Todd fitted Zip's mask first and then his own. They all went through their final equipment check. As they approached the drop zone, Fox and Penman helped strap Zip to Todd. When everything was set, the back of the aircraft opened and the coldest slap of wind he'd ever felt hit Zip in the face. His body stiffened and Todd felt his muscles contract. The team moved into position and when the red light went green, Fox flew out the door, followed Radar. They would be the first on the ground, and would mark the landing area for the rest of the team.

The remaining members of the team filed out of the plane in short order, until it was just Zip and Todd.

"Steady, Boy," he said, "we got this."

And then they were falling. The sound of the engines subsided quickly and all that was left was the whoosh of cold, rushing wind. Zip remained glued to Todd, and Todd could feel him panting as they plummeted toward the ground. Todd wanted to give him a reassuring hug, but he had work to do to ensure they remained stable through the freefall, and within close proximity of the rest of the team. As they neared the ground, Todd could see Fox and Penman's open chutes, and then watched them hit the ground. Quickly, green smoke marked the landing area. Todd steered them toward the smoke. He quickly checked his altimeter—900 feet. He pulled the ripcord. The sudden jolt was fierce. He and Zip had been falling at a rate of nearly 120 miles per hour when their descent was broken and slowed to twenty. Zip wasn't ready for it and the extreme deceleration knocked the wind out of him. When he and Todd hit the ground, he couldn't move, paralyzed by the lack of air caused by the sudden contraction of his diaphragm. Todd immediately knew something was wrong, disconnected his chute, and moved Zip to a prone position. Doc Burk saw what was going on and was there before Todd had a chance to call out for help.

"Doc, what is it?"

What had he done? Did he not check Zip's oxygen? Was there a problem with the harness?

"Give him a second," Doc answered dryly.

The team gathered around, staring at Zip and Doc. Doc grabbed Zip around the chest and sat with him between his legs. Zip was conscious but frozen. Doc gently began to squeeze Zip's chest to make his diaphragm relax. Soon, Zip felt the air flow back to his lungs, and he began to move his legs and started to pant.

Everyone on the team breathed with him.

Lieutenant Kelly observed the scene from a distance. His team had lost focus. They were watching a dog rather than deploying and securing the drop zone. R.J. was the first to come to his senses.

"Angel! Get to that ridge and check for movement," R.J. barked as he unpacked his radio. "Fox, get over here and help me establish comms."

He looked over at Lieutenant Kelly, realizing that he had made a critical mistake. This was all too little, too late. In a real situation the delay could jeopardize the team and mission.

In the past, military animals were pieces of equipment, nothing more. Since the time of the cavalry when thousands of horses were killed during charges or mules sacrificed in dangerous work, the U.S. armed forces realized that emotional attachments to animals had to be minimized. Many MWDs had been abandoned in Vietnam. Even if the attitudes were beginning to change, Kelly's team, and Todd Mitchell in particular, had developed an unhealthy fondness for a piece of military equipment. This was a dilemma for Lieutenant John Kelly. He liked that fur-ball too.

Chapter 5
A Guardian to My Fellow Americans

The training at Base Little Creek was nearly complete and Todd was given a two-week leave to go home to be with Lindsey who, now well into her third trimester, was expected to give birth any day. As soon as they got permission, Todd and Zip jumped into the Wrangler just after daybreak and started the seven-hour drive up to Burgettstown. Zip loved riding in the Jeep and the fall weather made the temperature just right. The smells were spectacular. Todd left the top down as they drove through the unusually warm morning. Zip could pick up the smells of the different trees, the goldenrod, and the scent of animals as they drove along the edge of the Monongahela National Forest on their way home. The trees were at their glorious peak of color and, while Zip couldn't completely appreciate the nuances of color, it appeared that Todd was enjoying the sights immensely. Zip found the beauty of this time of year in the wind that brought all the rich, telling scents of the forest to him.

It was a little after 1:00 p.m. when they turned off Route 18 and on to the tree-lined country road that lead to the Little R Dairy

Farm. Zip's nose was as high as it could go as he took in the sights and smells of the farm. As they pulled onto the gravel space outside the small but cozy farm house, Lindsey heard the crunch of the Jeep tires and came out onto the porch. Her belly was so large, she looked like she was about to pop but she moved with lightness and grace as she rushed to meet her husband. She threw her arms around his neck and kissed him passionately. Even though they had dated since they were seventeen and were well into their second year of marriage, they still felt the tingle of newlyweds whenever they could be together.

Zip ran up onto the porch fascinated with the new environment. This was new ground for him and he had to make sure everything was secure. He looked out over the barns and feed silos and at the main house just fifty yards away. Quickly he determined there was no real threat and turned his attention to Todd and Lindsey.

"And who is this?" Lindsey said as she looked at the bushy-tailed dog on her porch.

"Lindsey, meet Zip. Zip, this is Lindsey."

Zip walked up to Lindsey with his head high and his tail in the air. Lindsey bent down and gave him a big hug. Even though she wore no makeup or perfume, she smelled very nice—completely different than the people in his team. An instant feeling of comfort came over him and he rubbed his head against Lindsey's stomach. At that moment, the baby kicked and Zip jumped back, startled.

"Did you feel that?" Lindsey said laughing.

Zip tilted his head to one side like he always did when he was trying to size up a situation.

Todd said, "Don't worry, Boy. That's just your little sister."

The remark caught Lindsey off guard. *Little sister?* That was interesting. This was her husband's K9 partner. Zip didn't belong to him and she certainly didn't think the Navy would approve of Todd treating Zip like a pet, much less a member of his family. But there it was. Todd and Zip had already formed a very strong bond. Lindsey knew her husband had a knack for keeping everyone off guard—even the U.S. Navy.

Within a couple of minutes, Lindsey's grandfather stepped out from one of the barns.

"Hey Froggy!" Stan Ruddy bellowed from just outside the giant barn door. "Whacha got there with you?"

Stan ambled up to Todd and grabbed his hand in a firm shake that quickly dissolved into a sincere hug.

"Pap," Todd started again with the introductions, "This is Zip."

"Kind of small isn't he?" Stan said with a wide grin.

"You should see him work. Pap, I have never seen an animal quite like this."

"That's good," Stan said looking down at Zip. "You better take care of this one, you hear me, Boy? He's gonna be a daddy!"

From the main house, Val Ruddy watched the happy reunion and stepped out on the big porch to holler across the yard, "Who's hungry?"

Todd sprinted across the grass and bounded up the steps to pick up Grandma Val and swing her around in a massive hug.

Todd again introduced Zip and they all went into the big old house where Lindsey's mother had grown up. Val had prepared a magnificent lunch. A platter of cold ham surrounded by bowls of potato salad, bean salad, sweet corn, and fresh biscuits graced the kitchen table. Two berry pies were cooling on the counter. Emily lay under the table and barely even moved when everyone entered the house. She was a massive Newfoundland/English Mastiff mix, and she was no watchdog. Zip stopped and looked at her before walking over. Emily stood up and they greeted each other in the ways that dogs do. Emily very quickly indicated that she had had enough of the greeting and plopped herself down on her bed over near the pantry. Grandma Val fixed Zip a bowl of Emily's kibble and a fresh bowl of water, and they all sat down for lunch.

Later that afternoon, Shane and Jessica Wagner came out to the farm and Todd introduced Zip to Lindsey's parents. Then, just before dinner, Bob and Joan Mitchell arrived to join the party and they went through the entire process of introduction again. Val was in her bliss as the group ate dinner and voiced their appreciation of her cooking skills. They laughed, cracked a couple beers and caught up well into the night.

During a lull in the festivities, Todd walked out on the front porch to get some air with Zip by his side. As soon as they stepped outside, Todd's body reflexively went rigid as the smell of cherry blend pipe tobacco hit him. Ever since he was a boy, Bob Mitchell had smoked the same brand. It signaled his presence and Todd always associated the smell with a prelude to some lecture or other serious conversation.

"Nice night, eh Son?" Bob said from a dark corner of the porch. The orange glow from the bowl of his pipe gave the only indication of his location. "Nasty front is going to move through here later though."

"Hey Dad." Todd replied. "Yeah, I heard that on the news. The weather really can change quickly around here." Todd was trying to think of a way to keep the conversation away from controversy, but he knew it would only be a matter of time.

"Listen." Bob started.

"*Here we go.*" Todd said to himself and took a swig from his bottle of Rolling Rock to prepare for what was coming.

"First of all, I want you to know that I'm proud of you. Frankly, I never thought you'd make it through BUD/S but you always did have a way of surprising me. You've done well, but how long do you plan on doing this? I mean, now you're running around out there with a dog. Isn't that Boomer guy enough for you?"

Todd chuckled a little, being both amused and insulted at the same time by the back-handed complement and shots at his teammates.

"I guess not." Todd replied. "I like my team Dad. And I like what I do. Honestly, I can't understand why you like what you do. You dance around the fringes of the law making arguments for whoever can pay you four hundred bucks an hour. There's no right or wrong there—only defendants, plaintiffs and settlement dollars. You tell a story, they tell a story and then you sit in a back room and decide who told the best story and how many zeros go on the check. Either way, you get paid. What I do is focused. There are clear objectives and singularity of purpose. No manipulation or gray areas."

"Heh," Bob scoffed. "That's not exactly how it goes in my business Todd and I think you're being a bit naïve. You're a tool for the ideologues who see every problem as a nail in need of a hammer. You speak of singularity of purpose. Well, I don't know what you've seen in those other deployments Son, but it appears you've been lucky and I pray it stays that way for you. But I doubt it will. There's going to come a time when right, wrong, objective, duty and honor all get jumbled and tested in the blink of an eye. Do you know how you will handle that? The best of men seldom do."

He continued, "We have sacrificed at that alter already. Your

Great Uncle Ed was killed in Bastogne. Do you remember the Haddads? They have been family friends for years. Their son returned from Vietnam a completely changed man. It was as if someone else had been put in his body. He eventually put a bullet in his head to make the screaming stop. I know that we don't see eye-to-eye on many things but that doesn't mean I don't love you. You're a good man Todd. I know that. Please don't ever take our differences for anything other than what they are—differences."

Then he stood up and walked over to Todd and embraced him. "This whole situation over there is a mess Son. We need to get out. You've got too much to lose now. We need you to come back to us the good, strong person you have always been." He stepped back, wiped the tears from his eyes and cleaned his pipe by banging it against the porch post and walked back inside.

Todd took a seat on the porch steps to finish his beer and Zip came to his side. "That's the first time I've ever seen him cry." He said to Zip putting his arm around him.

Zip spent most of the rest of the evening observing the festivities and watching Emily sleep. As the night wore on, he again walked out onto the front porch of the main house and began to surveil the area around the farm. He could hear and smell the cows in the barns, and the other livestock settling down for the night. He felt his prey drive urge him to pursue that rabbit squeezing through a small fence opening near the garden. But he held his ground, knowing that his training only permitted an attack on command. The sights and sounds and smells of this place were what dog dreams were made of. Above all, Zip was drawn to the peacefulness of it all. He had never before experienced the kind of calmness as in this place.

Later that night, the warmth of the day gave way to a chill as the front Bob talked about swept through the area and dropped the temperature by a full thirty degrees. The wind kicked up and thumped tree branches against the little house. Todd and Lindsey lay covered in a thick comforter and Zip stayed positioned at the foot of the bed, curled on an old blanket, listening to the sounds of the wind gusts. As the temperature dropped, the furnace kicked on and warmth wafted up from the floor. Zip moved himself over to the furnace grate and plopped himself down, half covering it. The whisper of toasty air flowing up from the basement calmed him and drowned out the blowing wind.

The next morning, Todd was up and moving at 0630. The SEALs had taught him to rise early and, even on days he could sleep in, there was something that nudged him from rest and into being productive. While Lindsey still slept, he changed into sweatpants, a Penguins sweatshirt, and pulled on a wool cap marked with the SEAL trident. He looked over at Zip and made the soft clicking noise he used to call Zip when he wanted him to come quietly. Zip popped up from his spot near the register and tiptoed out with Todd to the front porch. The morning air was cold and there was moisture on the ground from when the front moved through. Zip scanned the farm grounds and noticed the mist of the morning and the first signs of daylight as the black of night transformed to the gray of morning and shades began to appear. Todd stepped off the porch and broke into a trot and Zip gave chase. Lately, Todd had gotten into the habit of letting Zip operate off his lead more than he should, which was another breach of Navy protocol. But Todd could count on Zip and, aside from Zip's predilection for lounging on furniture, found him to be completely disciplined when it came to obeying commands. He trusted his partner.

Zip was on the best run of his life. They ran through the woods along a trail and down to the edge of a wide lake that served as one of the county's reservoirs. The breaking daylight, crunching leaves, bird calls, and fascinating smells hanging in the still, damp air put him in a state of heightened awareness. After running for a full forty-five minutes, they stopped at a rock point on a ridge that overlooked a valley and the rolling hills of Western Pennsylvania; a spectacular view. Zip sat quietly at Todd's side, watching him watch the sun rise. The dampness was lifting and it would be a crisp fall day.

Todd sat down and rubbed Zip under his chin. Then he breathed a deep, uncharacteristic sigh. The silence between them and the start of a new day made him pensive. The weight of his new responsibilities, the unknowns of fatherhood, and the fact that he now had to make decisions beyond those selfish and foolish conveniences of his youth had been sinking in for days. The conversation with his dad and seeing him weep for the first time gave him a completely different perspective of his father. Todd needed someone to be there while he worked through it all—not to fix anything or do anything in particular—just to listen. Having Zip next to him somehow made him feel cared for, supported, and understood. After it all poured out of him, he sat there for thirty minutes without uttering another sound. Zip sat upright like a sentry, his breath condensing in the cold air. Then Todd snapped out of it, as if he had figured everything out.

"OK, Boy. Let's head on back and get some breakfast!"

And just like that, Todd was off again and Zip right along with him.

When they got back to the farm, Emily was out in the driveway and managed a half-hearted howl that wouldn't intimidate anything. Lindsey was up and over at the main house finishing a cup of decaf, while Stan was already out tending to the animals. Val fixed Todd a plate of bacon and eggs and served it up with a steaming cup of black coffee. Zip slurped at the bowl of water that Val had ready for him, getting more of it on the floor than in his mouth. Then she poured the last of the bacon drippings over his bowl of dog food. Zip ate like he had missed a week of meals, pounding the stainless steel bowl against the wall with his nose as he licked up every morsel.

Later that day, Todd, Val, and Lindsey drove up to Robinson Township to pick up some more baby supplies and a few last pieces of layette. They left Zip with Stan to run the farm. Stan took Zip outside and let him go into the barns to see the livestock. He was fascinated with the way that Zip seemed to want to go to work. Stan kept a number of goats and sheep in a one-acre pen outside the main barn that were presently holding Zip's attention. Stan hesitated a bit and then opened the pen gate to see what Zip would do. Zip flew through the open gate and Stan gasped, thinking he had made a terrible mistake and that Zip was going to attack the livestock. Zip flew at tremendous speed, closing ground between him and the bleating sheep in seconds. Just when he looked like he would pounce on the animal furthest outside the herd, Zip spun sharply to his right. As the lone sheep scampered farther away from the group, Zip cut him off and drove him back to the flock.

"Well I'll be damned," Stan muttered to himself as he watched Zip instinctively run circles around the goats and sheep, keeping them in a tight group. Once Zip was sure he had them all together, he jumped up on a stump that Stan used to chop logs and surveyed "his" herd. Stan was surprised by Zip's speed, but his drives to cut across the sheep paths in anticipation of their movements astonished him. Todd was right. This dog was special. Stan looked down at Emily who had wandered up next to him in order to get a better view of all the commotion.

"Why can't you do that?" he said.

Emily moaned and draped her huge head over a strand of pen wire, and then let out a deep sigh to let him know that she couldn't care less.

Late in the afternoon, everyone returned and Val pulled a pot of stew off the stove that had been simmering all day. Beef stew and biscuits were on the menu tonight and Todd's parents once again came to join them for dinner. After a couple of rounds of Euchre and more reminiscing, things broke up around 11:00 p.m. The Mitchells had just pulled away when Lindsey felt the first contraction. It was hard. Her water broke and she knew that it was time. Todd went into command mode.

But Zip sat in the corner, confused by the orderly chaos. Lindsey seemed to be hurt and upset, and everyone was doing something quickly. Todd was ignoring him. This was obviously an important mission. Why wasn't he being told what to do? Why wasn't he part of this team? He looked at Emily, then crawled under the table to lie next to her. Maybe this was the best place to be right now.

Todd called the Mitchells back to the house and got the Wagners on the phone, and before long a small convoy was off for the hospital. Stan and Val stayed behind to man the phones and keep coffee on. They made sure Zip had plenty of water and had been taken out and left him in the small house by himself.

In the early hours of the following morning, Lindsey and Todd welcomed Caroline Katherine Mitchell into the world. Todd could not have been prouder and held his little girl for as long as he possibly could before the nurses made him give her up so mother and daughter could get some rest. Satisfied that his girls would be taken care of, he finally came back to the farm in the middle of the afternoon and greeted Zip with a giant hug and a short wrestling match. Val had left him a plate of warmed-over stew and a note to call if he needed anything. It was Great Gran and Gramp's turn to see the new baby. Exhausted, he fell asleep on the couch watching the Pitt football game, with a great big smile on his face.

Zip never saw Todd so happy. He paced through each of the rooms of the small farm house one more time before taking up a position between Todd and the front door. They both slept soundly.

Two days later, it was time for Lindsey and Caroline to come home from the hospital. Val and Stan made a small homecoming reception for them and then left the new family alone to get acquainted. Todd made one more introduction to Zip.

"Hey, Boy," Todd whispered. "This is your little sister, Caroline. She's very small now and not much fun. But someday you two are going to be great friends."

Something came over Zip when he saw the baby. He had never felt a stronger protective urge. He didn't know why, only that he could never let any harm come to this little thing. During her first full day at home, Zip refused to leave Caroline's side. He followed Lindsey wherever she took the baby, always setting up station between the mother, daughter, and nearest access point into the room. Any threat moving toward the two of them would have to get through him first. During the first night, Lindsey was sleeping soundly when Todd awoke, surprised to find Zip missing from the foot of the bed. He padded down the hall to Caroline's room next to theirs. There was Zip, positioned directly underneath the crib with an overview of the entire room, his head covered in shadows. Todd smiled and returned to bed. Each time Caroline moved or began to fuss, Zip was back in their bedroom, nudging Todd or Lindsey to attend to her needs.

This was the process for the next several nights. Todd even had trouble getting Zip out on their morning runs. After a week, it was time for Todd and Zip to head back to the base. Todd knew another deployment was coming and was finding it hard to break away this time. Zip was finding it harder. When the jeep was packed and everything was together, Todd gave Lindsey and Caroline a final kiss goodbye and called for Zip. There was no response.

Zip sat motionless on the porch. He could not figure out why Todd would want to leave this place, and he certainly didn't want to go. Todd whistled and snapped at him. "Zip! Let's go! We're going to be AWOL." Zip didn't budge.

Lindsey walked up to Zip with Caroline in her arms and bent over and whispered to him, "Look Zip, you need to go with Todd. We'll be fine. He needs you now. We will all be waiting for you when you get back, but right now you need to take care of Todd for all of us." She cradled Caroline next to him, and hugged him around his neck with her free arm, "Now go do your job."

Zip looked at Lindsey and licked her face and sniffed at Caroline, licking the top of her head.

One last time Todd called for Zip and he reluctantly trotted off the porch and up into the passenger seat of the Jeep. Todd walked back and hugged everyone again, with one last stop for Lindsey and Caroline.

"I love you," he said, gazing at them together.

"We know." Lindsey grabbed him around the neck and kissed him, battling back the tears. "You have a good partner. Now go on and look out for each other and don't do anything stupid."

Todd jumped into the Jeep, slid on his sun glasses, and threw his shoulders back. "Let's go to work," he said to Zip as he put the vehicle in gear and they pulled out of the drive.

Lindsey could no longer keep up the brave smile, and she began to sob as she watched the Jeep drive out of sight.

Chapter 6
I Serve With Honor on and off the Battlefield

The Korengal Valley in the northeastern portion of Afghanistan, Kunar Province, had been the center of the most intense fighting of the Afghan engagement. More American blood had been spilled there than in any other location in Afghanistan. This is where the First Squad of the Second Platoon of SEAL Team 4 would call home for a large portion of their forward deployment. The mountainous area was naturally covered in pines, but large areas had been stripped of tree canopy by logging operations. The beautiful, rugged area bred hard people.

The team's first stop in Afghanistan was Bagram Air Base. The massive military complex run by the U.S. Air Force was populated with all of the forces of the U.S. and coalition military. The airfield was one of the main operating posts for all military operations of the International Security Assistance Force (ISAF) assigned to operation Enduring Freedom. This was the second time the team had spent time at Bagram, so they knew their way around pretty well. It was harder for Zip.

Zip spent much of his first week on the base trying to get

himself used to the strange new surroundings. His body needed to adjust its internal clock. Being a full nine and a half hours ahead of Virginia time really messed him up, and it took him days to fall into regular eating and sleeping cycles. During the long series of flights over a two-day period he was sedated, which didn't help his adjustment to this curious land. The familiarity of military surroundings helped him to adjust somewhat, but the general atmosphere of this cold and barren land was something that he was having trouble getting used to.

The rest of the team was also adjusting in their own ways. Lieutenant Kelly spent most of his time with the Company Commander, Navy Commander Mathew D. Heard. R.J. was catching up on his workouts and trying out Bagram's gym, thoroughly impressing everyone on base in the process. Angel took time to evaluate the weapons inventory and study the maps and terrain of the valley with Fox. Boomer and Todd scrounged for supplies, especially trying to accumulate as much junk food as they possibly could move forward with as well as the special food that Zip would need in the tough mountain terrain. Penman set about getting to know the team's newest member, their Afghan interpreter.

Abdul "Abby" Ashkilani would be assigned to SEAL Team 4 during their time in the Korengal. He was a tough man who looked significantly older than his forty years. From the time he was a small boy, there had been some sort of war raging in his land, and the permanent state of conflict had hardened him both physically and emotionally. Although he had a Persian name, he was actually Tajik. His father had fought with the Mujahideen against the Soviet invasion in the 1980s and had survived only to become completely disillusioned with the results. Although the Mujahideen were successful at repelling the communist invaders, it allowed another, equally oppressive group to rise in place of the Russians. The Taliban was not what Ghazi Ashkilani had in mind for himself or his family as a reward for what he viewed as a glorious victory in the name of Allah.

The bitterness flowed from father to son. Ghazi had worked closely with CIA operatives during the time of the Soviet invasion, helping to smuggle Stinger missiles through the Khyber Pass and into the Hindu Kush Mountains. He brought his young son with him and Abby quickly became acquainted with the ways of the CIA and Special Forces operatives who were secretly working with the Mujahideen. The Americans taught him English, even as he cultivated his skills in Russian, Dari, and his native Pashto. Now, this linguistic proficiency made him a very valuable asset to the ISAF forces.

During a brief period of peace before the Taliban regime was fully able to exert its influence, Abby married and they had three daughters. Bibi Kur was Abby's devoted wife. She was resilient, and as strong as Abby. She understood the sacrifices that had been made by Ghazi Ashkilani and by her own family as well. She had lost both parents during the Soviet invasion, and it was Ghazi's family who took her in and protected her. Bibi knew her daughters would never achieve their potential living under Taliban rule, so she supported Abby in the fight against oppression. She also knew that she could lose her husband in the process, and not only in the physical sense.

Abby's daughters were beautiful, intelligent, and strong-willed, independent thinkers—a recipe for disaster with the Taliban. Abby and Bibi Kur knew this and worried constantly for them.

The eldest and smartest was Zohal. Wise and compassionate beyond her eighteen years, she aspired to become a doctor. She had already seen so much pain in her life and the lives of others, and she wanted to do something about it. Zahmina Rai was the middle child and the athlete in the family. She loved to dance and was an excellent soccer player. When she was younger, she cut her hair short and disguised herself as a boy so that Bibi Kur could sneak her into neighboring villages to play soccer with the boys. The consequences of being discovered by the Taliban could have been deadly for them both, and Bibi sometimes wondered what she was thinking by allowing it. The youngest and most rebellious of the sisters was Shaima. At only thirteen years, she was already stubbornly refusing to wear a chador or even a hijab. Abby, Bibi, and her sisters knew she would surely become a target of the fundamentalists if she did not learn to keep her head covered and her mouth shut.

And so, Abby quietly snuck his family out of Kabul and moved them to the small city of Chehl Sutoon in the western plains of the country where the Taliban still had little influence. He then went back to the mountains where he joined the Northern Alliance, a loose network of Afghan tribes that had come together to resist the

Taliban. The NA realized that the Taliban was nothing more than a power hungry, tyrannical political group hiding behind their own hypocritical interpretation of Sharia Law. Abby scoffed at the notion of ever having to live under those that would pervert the words of Allah and the teachings of the Prophet in such a way. Even the name "Taliban" turned his stomach. The Pashto word "Talib" means "seeker of knowledge." In Abby's mind, these were the last people on earth looking to be enlightened.

Now he was here, working with the ISAF forces and meeting his new team. He knew the mountains and the various villages and tribes in the area; he knew those that were sympathetic to the remnants of the Northern Alliance, those that were indifferent, and those out for a profit. All of them had a role to play in Abby's personal fight. He met regularly with Commander Heard and Lieutenant Kelly to give them intelligence on the area, but he spent most of his time with Penman. The two connected with their passion for language. Before long, Abby was sincerely impressed with Penman's ability to pick up on the regional dialect and accents as he reviewed the differences in Arabic, Pashto and Dari. Soon, the two were holding rapid conversations mixing all three together, as well as a little Russian thrown into the mix.

Around the end of their first week on base, Abby got his things together and moved over to the barracks with the rest of the team. Penman, who was helping him load his stuff, entered first to open the door wide and hold it for him, but Abby stopped dead in his tracks at the threshold.

"There is an animal in here," he said in disbelief as he spotted Zip on Todd's bunk.

"Oh, that's just Zip," Penman said. "He's part of the team."

Zip was sprawled as usual across Todd's rack and took little notice of Abby as he took one, and only one, step into the room.

Abby stared at Zip intently and said nothing for an uncomfortably long period of time until he finally uttered, "The other dogs on this base are not in barracks. Dogs do not belong in the same living quarters with humans."

"Well, this one does," Penman said. "What the hell is wrong with you, anyway?"

"Dogs do not belong in the same living quarters with humans," Abby repeated. Then he promptly spun on his heel and left.

Penman was not happy with the tension created between them,

but losing an interpreter was the bigger problem, so he tracked down both Lieutenant Kelly and Todd immediately to explain what had happened. Todd was pissed.

"Screw him!"

"Shut up Mitchell!" Kelly snapped back, his tenor reaching the top of its register. "Look stupid, you have pushed the limits with that dog and if it comes down to a choice between our interpreter and that mutt, guess who wins? I'll put him out in the kennels and that will be the end of it! Is that clear to you, Petty Officer?"

Mitchell was still defiant and responded in typical smart-ass fashion, "Oh, come on now Lieutenant, this *is* their country. I don't think you need to put the towel head out in the kennel, it just wouldn't be right."

"Are you done pushing me?" Kelly glared.

Todd knew he had better gear down and backed off. "Yes Sir. Sorry, Sir."

"Now go work this thing out. If you can't, *Zip* goes to the kennel. Got it?"

"Yes Sir." Todd turned without another word and headed briskly out the door of the command post.

"What the hell is wrong with that guy?" Todd asked Penman as they walked back to the barracks.

"Come on Todd, this isn't your first rodeo over here," Penman said. "You know Muslims don't keep animals in the house, especially dogs. They think they're unclean, and exist only for work and protection. These guys don't keep pets. Most of the dogs in this country are half wild and full of disease. Besides, Abby's never seen a dog like Zip. In his head, all the military working dogs are just trained killers. Look, you're going to have to convince this guy. I'll help you. He's really sharp and one tough SOB. I think you'll like him."

"Dogs are filthy and never permitted in the house?" Todd replied. "Have you looked around this place? There isn't a clean spot in this whole wasteland of a country. I mean, look at it! The entire damn country is gray! The houses are gray, the ground is gray, the sky is gray, hell, even the people are gray! Well, I better like him; and he better come around because Zip isn't going anywhere."

When they got back to the barracks, Abby was standing at near attention with his gear neatly placed beside him. Todd called Zip and he trotted from the barracks and sat down beside him.

"You're Abby Ashkilani. It's a pleasure to meet you," Todd said in the most diplomatic voice he could muster. I've heard a lot about you in the short time we have been here and I know we'll work well together."

Penman fought the urge to roll his eyes, and had trouble hiding his incredulity at Todd's line of BS.

"Thank you, Petty Officer," Abby said. "It is also a pleasure to meet you and an honor to work with such a group of distinguished warriors." This was Abby's own line of BS. He had seen everything from Soviet Spetsnaz, to British SAS Commandoes to Norwegian FSK. He had been on deployment with U.S. Army Rangers and Delta Force personnel but he had never worked with SEALs before and, though he knew the reputation, they would still have to prove themselves if they were going to gain Abby Ashkilani's respect.

They moved to a picnic table alongside the barracks and Penman diplomatically brought tea for them. Zip sat up straight by Todd's side, keeping a watchful eye on this new person. For the first few minutes, Abby had trouble concentrating on what was being said because he was continually distracted by the animal that seemed to be listening to him as intently as Todd and Penman were.

The three men talked for an hour. Todd explained the situation with Zip—how he was part of a fairly new program—and described the dog's training. He pointed out that Zip served many purposes, and was not trained only to pursue and attack. He let Abby know that Zip needed to be in such close contact with the team so they could learn each other's mannerisms and develop a nonverbal form of communication, and that he, in particular, needed to gauge how Zip might react in stressful situations.

Boomer came back from his workout about then and joined them, bringing some nuts and dates to have with the remaining tea. He opened a can of Pringles for himself.

Throughout the course of the conversation, Abby tried to relax. He could see that Todd was speaking with complete sincerity and could sense that this man and this dog had a bond beyond others. Now it was Abby's took turn to explain his objection to the cohabitation.

"You see, gentlemen," he began, "I have never kept company

with these animals for any particular amount of time, other than to run from them. When I was a child, I watched the dogs of the Soviet Army tear apart women and children even younger than myself. They terrorized us looking for Mujahideen. Many of the Soviet Spetsnaz forces used dogs bred at the Red Star Kennels." Abby saw Todd's right eyebrow go up. "You've heard of this place, yes? I have heard that they were known to genetically experiment with various breeds of dogs. Some of those Soviet military dogs had the blood of fifteen or twenty different breeds, including the wolf breeds. They made these dogs vicious. They were trained to intimidate us.

"When I was thirteen, my cousin and I, who was eleven, were watching the fence line of a Soviet encampment. Our job was to focus on the main gate and report to my uncle when patrols left the camp. One night, the guards spotted us and began to chase us with their dogs. We ran and ran like the wind, but still they chased us until we came to a dead end and they had us pinned against the wall of a courtyard. I was taller and stronger than my cousin and was able to leap and pull myself to the top of the wall."

Abby stopped for a moment and looked down at his boots. "But my cousin was not reaching the top. I leaned over to help him and had him by the wrist but the dogs grabbed him and my grip failed. Two of these beasts pulled him to the ground and were on him. I sat there, on the other side of the wall, listening to those Soviet bastards laugh at my cousin's screams, until he stopped screaming and they pulled the dogs away. They thought my cousin was dead, or dying, so they left him there.

"When I was sure they were gone, I climbed back over the wall and somehow managed to carry my cousin back to my uncle, his father. Rakeem was permanently blinded and lost the use of one arm. He cannot work or have a normal life. He lives with hideous scars and wakes in terror, still hearing the dogs when he sleeps. Sometimes I hear them, too." Abby brought his eyes back up and looked over the table at Todd. "Dogs are the weapon of a coward."

Todd, Penman, and Boomer sat in stunned silence as Abby finished his story. Todd began to get a better understanding of the man and a measure of respect. Later, as the course of the conversation lightened, they exchanged personal anecdotes. Abby told Todd of his three daughters and Todd told Abby that he was a new father to a daughter. Abby smiled and began to talk of the difficulties of rearing women and what Todd was destined for. In the end, the two came to an agreement about Zip. Abby would stay in the farthest bunk from Zip, and Zip would not be permitted to cross the barracks to Abby's side. Todd would train Zip to have no personal contact with Abby. Zip would not approach him for any reason. It was a workable compromise.

The team spent another full month at Bagram riding out the bulk of the winter. When eventually deployed into the Korengal Valley, the platoons would take turns spending a month at a combat outpost (COP). First Platoon would be deployed to the Korengal first, while Second Platoon stayed at Bagram to review additional intelligence and continue training. Zip and the team passed the days before deployment becoming acclimated to the area. The SEALs reviewed intelligence reports from Naval Intelligence, CIA operatives, and other operational summaries as they gathered further information on their mission.

It was clear to them that Afghanistan was never going to become a true democracy. The country and its people were too hardened by nearly two thousand years of war and invasions to really trust any form of centralized government, or embrace the concept of democratic freedom as an institutional ideal. What could be trusted was the loyalty of a tribe or particular ethnic group. The ISAF intelligence community had realized this long ago. The best they could hope for was to institute an oxymoronic concept of "ordered anarchy" in the region.

The premise was not as crazy as it sounded. ISAF let the local tribes know that they had no intention of imposing democracy or any ideology on the people of the Hindu Kush. Their aim was to strengthen the individuality of the region and establish a network of communication between each tribe. By doing this, they could set up a loose conglomeration of city- or tribe-states that could trade and interact while remaining separate in their traditions. The hope was to make the tribes interdependent. Then, anytime an imposing force would intrude, or seek to assimilate them into a greater whole, the tribes could come together to uniformly negotiate or resist. It was a struggle for the soul of the Hindu Kush. Cooperation, interdependence, hope, commerce, education, and opportunity were kryptonite to the Taliban and they were prepared to subvert any attempts at such by the ISAF.

The Taliban was a formidable foe. They weren't stupid and they had the supreme confidence that the power of God was on their side. There was no way that the infidels, with their lack of conviction, could possibly win in this holy battle for *their* people. However, even the mullahs who had spent years studying in the Pakistani madrassas could not easily overcome the cynicism of a tribal elder. Still, the Taliban were well entrenched and had their sympathizers. There were many who had been indoctrinated to hate all that the West represented, and viewed this latest effort as just another crusade to draw them further from the rule of Allah and the teachings of the Prophet.

In this struggle, the role of Navy SEAL Team 4 and other combat troops in the area was relatively straight forward, but incredibly difficult. They were to root out the Taliban and dilute their influence for as long as possible while fostering a system of cooperation and commerce. The concept was that by providing stability and strengthening the local economy, they would diminish opportunities for fanaticism and the subsequent development of terrorism. Unfortunately, time was not on the ISAF's side. Troop drawdowns had already begun, impacting their efforts. The long process of gaining tribal trust could quickly erode.

Chapter 7
The Execution of My Duties

Two weeks before the squads were scheduled to be deployed to the Korengal Valley and their designated combat outpost, Commander Heard unexpectedly called the men of the Second Platoon together in the Situation Room assigned to the SEALs and the Joint Special Operations Command near the SEAL Team Barracks at Bagram.

"Gentlemen this is Jennifer Kennedy. Her name doesn't matter because she doesn't exist anyway. We have some work to do before you head to the field."

Without waiting for further introduction, Kennedy stepped in front of the group. She pressed a remote control and a picture of an ordinary looking Afghani or Pakistani man appeared on the middle screen of the three TVs at the front of the room.

"This is Kahlil Gul," She began. "He is one of the chief financiers for the Taliban and he is paying a visit to Kabul tomorrow. We have reliable intel that gives us his time and a meeting point. You are going to get him for us. Commander Heard will give you all the ops detail."

Kennedy stepped to the side and Heard again moved to the

front of the room. "This is going to be a quick grab. Intelligence has learned that there is a group of Saudis and Pakistanis that have a vested interest in continuing to finance the Tali. We know that Gul is the guy taking the funds and funneling them through various Swiss and Cayman accounts. He then moves the money to a group of former KGB and Chinese arms dealers. The weapons are then smuggled through Pakistan and into Afghanistan.

"Tomorrow, he is meeting with a Saudi contact that CIA has eyes on. When the meeting is done, the CIA will continue to tail the Saudi to gather further information on his network. He is not the target. We want Gul. He is near the end of his intelligence usefulness and it is time to bring him in for interrogation so CIA can glean further information from him and continue to piece together the Tali network in the country.

"This is what we are going to do. Once the meeting is finished, the intel contact in Kabul will confirm his exit route." He clicked the remote control and a map of Kabul appeared on the right-hand screen. "Our source tells us the meeting will be held near the northwest corner of the city. If correct, we will be able to catch him—here." He pointed to a circle on the map. "This is the intersection of Tajikan Road and Kohistan Road. This vacant lot to the west," he pointed to another circle, "is a great area to put a chopper down and whisk him away. It also gives our team an easy escape route out of the city. We will insert Second Squad to cut him off, snatch him off the street, and move him to the extraction point where the helo will be waiting to get him back here for interrogation. The Master Chief will lead the insertion team."

The Master Chief Petty Officer of whom Heard spoke was William "Wild Bill" Kerski. Todd knew him well, and he was one of the toughest SEALs he had ever met. Kerski was no-nonsense. Todd could never recall a time when he saw him smile. What he lacked in personality, he made up for with brilliant leadership, however, and he was beloved by the men of the Team. He constantly reminded them of their purpose and continually worked with all the men of the platoon on their combat skills and individual disciplines. Todd recalled once when Boomer was doing his usual "goofing off" act during a training exercise, Wild Bill got fed up hurled a Humvee tire at him. He was not a man to be trifled with. Boomer learned his lesson the hard way as it took a couple of weeks for the bruising on his chest to go away.

Commander Heard continued his briefing over the next hour. First Squad's role in the mission would be to act as backup, in case anything went wrong, and remain on standby at Bagram. Lieutenant Kelly would stay with Commander Heard in the situation room and R.J. would lead the reserve squad if they were called upon.

The Second Squad would be inserted just on the edge of Kabul near the intersection that Heard described. As Gul and his party approached the point, the CIA informant would give the word and Second Squad would block the path from both sides of the street with a couple of armored Mercedes SUVs, the type typically used as diplomatic transport. Once they had Gul, they would speed to the open field where the Blackhawk helicopter would be waiting to take Gul back to Bagram.

The Team held a final briefing the day of the operation. Second Squad would depart at 1100 in civilian clothing. First Squad would remain in uniform and ready if their backup was needed. They anticipated the Saudi meeting would be over sometime between afternoon and evening prayer when slightly less traffic could be expected. They were ready.

Second Squad departed in the SUVs to move to their intercept positions. The extraction Blackhawk and backup sat on the tarmac outside the situation room. Drone reconnaissance was deployed above the area of operation and Heard, Kennedy, and Kelly went to the Situation Room to watch the operation unfold.

First Squad waited outside hoping they would not be needed. While Angel, R.J., and Doc sprawled on lawn chairs, Radar and Fox dealt cards for rummy. Todd picked up a bat and tossed a whiffle ball at Boomer, who pitched while Penman acted as umpire and announcer. Zip stayed at Todd's side and each time he hit the ball, Zip sprinted after it, catching almost every fly ball before it hit the ground.

"Does he have to slobber all over it?" Boomer said as Zip retrieved another ball and returned it to him. Then he made a big gesture of wiping the ball and his hand off on his pants.

"Why does that bother you?" Todd said. "You're just using all that spit to put more spin on the ball anyway."

"Uhn-uh. That's all me, Son. No additives needed to strike you out."

Boomer wound up once again and delivered a pitch that Todd

nailed, and it shot out onto the tarmac too hard and too fast for Zip to catch this time.

"Eat that, Stocky!" Todd exclaimed as he flipped the bat and pretended to run the bases at a deliberate trot, staring Boomer down the whole time.

"Keep it up hot shot. The next one's coming straight for your head."

"Hey, quiet!" R.J. broke in, pointing to his radio headpiece. "Troops in contact! The grab went bad! Let's go!"

The squad grabbed their gear and headed to the helicopter, which was already powering up its engines. Todd and Zip were the first ones in. As the squad put on their headphones so they could be heard above the noise of the helicopter rotors, Angel started pressing R.J. for the details.

"What the hell happened?"

"Info's still coming in. Somehow the Tali got tipped off. They hit one of the SUVs with an RPG round and we have wounded. The second SUV with the Master Chief got cut off and they're in a firefight. We need to get the wounded out and get to the Chief."

"Who's with him?" Todd asked

"Hill and Raddock."

The helicopter made the trip to the edge of Kabul in under five minutes.

"Put us down as close to the action as you can," R.J. ordered the pilot.

The extraction helicopter moved in formation with the first and descended at the designated point. First Squad could now see the remainder of Second Squad; they had formed a makeshift perimeter and were fighting off a band of attacking insurgents. It looked like they were trying to advance and get to Kerski, Hill, and Raddock while dealing with their wounded. There was just no way they were going to leave without all of their team.

The Blackhawk touched down and First Squad immediately joined the fight.

"Check right!" R.J. said to Todd and Boomer as they bailed out of the helicopter with their weapons at the ready. The rest of the squad moved forward, ready to provide support.

The helicopter lifted back off and the side door gunner opened up with much-needed covering fire, allowing the first squad to reach the second.

"Status!" R.J. shouted at the Chief Petty Officer holding the second squad together.

"We've got a few scratches but we're going back for the Master Chief. He's trapped in that second building on the right. We saw at least ten of those bastards go in after him."

"Where's Gul?"

"Never saw him. They ambushed us just as we moved the SUVs into position. I doubt he was ever here."

"They've got more than scratches," Doc said as he worked to triage the wounded. "R.J., these guys can't fight. Look at 'em. I've got at least two fractures and one guy with arterial bleeding. The CPO's ear is barely hanging on his damned head."

"Copy that," R.J said as he turned back to the CPO. "Listen to me!" he screamed. "I'm taking over here. You get back to the extraction zone with Doc. He'll look after your team. We'll get the Master Chief."

"No way!" the CPO screamed back at him and again turned his attention to the building with the Master Chief.

"Look at your men! Look at them!" R.J. grabbed his shoulder and spun him around to see the carnage behind him. "You can't do anything more. You get them back or we'll need body bags."

He was done trying to bring the CPO to his senses and, without waiting for an answer, R.J. took over. "Doc, you and Fox get these guys back to the extraction point. See what you can do for them. Boomer and Todd, take Zip with you and head into that building. Find the Master Chief, Hill, and Raddock, and get them out of there. Penman and Angel will cover your entrance. Radar and I will provide cover from here while you're on the move and during evac. Now go!"

The squad was in motion before R.J. finished his sentence. The insurgents attacking Second Squad had backed off when they saw reinforcements arrive. Now the street was eerily quiet as the SEALs moved down past the burning SUVs to the identified building. It was an abandoned, two-story concrete building that looked as if it had been a small apartment complex at one time. When they got to the front entrance, they could see that the main door was barely hanging on the hinges. There was no noise coming from inside.

"Angel, you and Penman find some cover where you got eyes on the whole front of this building. Cut down anyone who tries to follow us," Boomer instructed.

"Copy that."

Boomer half-whispered to Todd and glanced down at Zip, "Let's go, quiet. If there's any left in there, let's not advertise ourselves."

Todd confirmed the instruction with a nod.

The front door was ajar and the three SEALs slipped through the entrance, disappearing into the darkness of the main hallway. Boomer put his fist in the air indicating a stop, to give them a minute for their eyes to adjust from the bright sunshine to the dimness of the windowless hallway where they now stood.

Zip and Todd paid attention to Boomer's hand signals and when they were ready to move again he led them stealthily through the first floor of the building. As they reached a staircase to the second floor, they saw insurgent bodies strewn about the steps. Slowly and gingerly the three tread over and around the bodies as they climbed the stairs, taking care to ensure there was no movement and no insurgent playing 'possum. Todd kept a silent count as they ascended into the second floor hallway. There were five combatant bodies in the stairwell and an additional three in the hall.

The doors to the vacant one-room apartments were slightly ajar. Todd motioned for Zip to push each open a little wider with his nose so they could get a better look inside as they made their way down the corridor. They saw no one, but the last two doors were completely closed. As they approached the second to last apartment, they could smell something burning and heard a hissing sound from inside. Boomer checked the door for heat and then tried the knob. The door was not locked. Boomer gave a silent count—one, two, three—and they rapidly shoved open the door and ducked inside with Boomer breaking left and Todd and Zip breaking right. Boomer swept the room, scanning each corner with his weapon at the ready, while Todd and Zip checked behind the door.

There were four bodies. One of them was Wild Bill. He sat propped up in a corner of the room with his eyes wide open, still looking straight at the entrance. Boomer kneeled and checked for a pulse. There was none. Todd and Zip assessed the others. They were all insurgents and they were all dead. One had two bullet wounds to his chest. The broken blade of a field knife protruded from the ribcage of another, and the last was smoldering. The fluorescent red flame of a signaling flare crackled and glowed from under what was left of his shirt, as the flare burned to its end. The smell coming from the body was putrid.

Boomer started to take account of the situation. "His weapon is empty," he said as he picked up Will Bill's handgun from the floor. "He must have used his last rounds on the guy by the door."

Todd rolled the second body on its side. "Looks like he broke his knife off in this one."

The three of them stood over the third body, but Zip backed away, annoyed by the smell and the hiss.

"What the hell did he do to this one?" Boomer said.

"Looks like he took him out with the only thing he had left. Look at his face. His eyes are nearly burnt away." Todd bent and picked up the Russian-made handgun lying next to the body. "This guy still has a couple rounds in his Makarov. The Master Chief must have already been shot when he took the guy down with him. Then he crawled back to the corner thinking he could still cover the entrance somehow."

"Jeezuhs," Boomer said. "But where the hell are Hill and Raddock?"

Zip wasn't paying attention to Todd or Boomer or the bodies on the floor anymore. He was staring out the open door and across the hallway. Then Todd heard it, too, and placed his fingers to his lips. A thumping sound was coming from the last closed apartment. Boomer and Todd immediately raised their weapons in response. They crept across the hallway and took positions outside the door and listened as the muffled pounding sound continued. Boomer nodded at Todd, who moved beside him, and then kicked open the door. Todd shot through, ready to fire at any threat.

Inside stood Jack Hill and Dan Raddock. They were startled when the door flew off its hinges and caught completely off guard when Todd, Zip, and Boomer charged in. They had been too engaged in what they were doing.

An Afghani girl, not more than sixteen or seventeen from the look of her, was curled in a ball on the floor beneath them. One eye, black and blue, was swollen shut. Ugly bruises covered her face and arms, there was a gash across her cheek, and blood ran from her nose and the corners of her mouth. She had obviously been beaten almost senseless.

"What the hell is going on here?" Todd screamed.

"Stay out of this Mitchell," Hill said through clenched teeth. "This doesn't concern you."

"The hell it doesn't!"

"This bitch set us up!" Raddock said angrily. "She spotted for them, gave the CIA the wrong route, and they were waiting for us with a decoy. She knew everything!"

The girl on the floor was a bloody mess. She raised one hand up and cried in pain, and in English, "No. No. Please!"

"How do you know that, Raddock?" Boomer said.

Hill spoke again. "It was obvious. When we got to the intercept point, she was supposed to ID Gul's car. The one she pointed out was full of Tali ready to hit us. They took out the back Mercedes with an RPG and then cut us off in the forward position. We barely made it inside when they sent those bastards out there after us. They threw a grenade down the hall and me and Dan jumped in here and the Master Chief in that room. This bitch just happened to be hiding in here after she tipped them off and obviously didn't know we would be coming. Now she's going to pay for what she did to us, for what she did to Wild Bill."

"Let her go," Todd said. "That story's weak. Let's get her back to Bagram and let them decide."

"Bullshit!" Hill screamed as he grabbed the moaning girl by the hair and pulled her up off the floor with one hand, his other fist raised to continue where they'd left off.

"Let her go, dammit!" Todd raised his voice and looked at Zip to signal an attack. "Let her go or I'll turn the dog loose on the both of you."

"You keep that hair missile away from me Mitchell. You're not stopping this."

Zip was confused but the hair on his back was up. He knew these men. They were part of his platoon. He had played with them and drilled with them back in Virginia and here in Afghanistan. He liked Hill and Raddock. He was about to receive a command to attack his own team.

Boomer, stunned, stood motionless. But when he saw that Todd was determined he took a step forward, and firmly put his arm across Todd's chest.

Todd looked at Boomer with more than a little surprise, and then he saw the look on his friend's face. Boomer believed Hill and Raddock.

Boomer looked Todd squarely in the eye and then shifted his gaze across to the room containing the Master Chief's body, and shook his head.

Todd stared back at Boomer for a second, looked down at Zip, and then exhaled deeply. Then he looked at Hill and Raddock, and finally at the girl. Her beaten face, filled with terror, pain, and desperation, silently pleaded for help.

Without a word, Todd spun toward the door and exited down the hallway, followed by Zip and Boomer. As they reached the top of the stairs, he heard the pounding start up again. He kept walking, eyes forward, Zip at his heel.

When they exited the building, Boomer signaled all clear. Angel and Penman left their cover and darted up to the three of them.

"The Master Chief is dead," Boomer said, jaw set. "Hill and Raddock are with him. They're OK. Stay here and cover the entrance. We're going to get a body bag."

As they left the other SEALs and began walking down the street, a single gunshot rang out from inside the building.

Chapter 8
The Inherent Hazards of My Profession

In the first week of March, their last week before deployment to the COP, the team conducted checks of their gear and received final intelligence briefings. Todd was able to get in a few Skype sessions with Lindsey and Caroline. He couldn't believe that his daughter was already five months old, and looked different every time he saw her in the streaming video. He had never felt homesick on other deployments. But this time he was missing his new family and it tore him apart.

He compensated by tightening his bond with Zip. They took long walks, shared exercise and Frisbee sessions, and Todd perfected his commands to ensure that everything Zip had learned became almost instinctive. Even though Todd had broken protocol—and some regulations—in cultivating his unique relationship with Zip, he made sure that the two were in complete sync with each other as they moved through their drills.

The team was deployed to Combat Outpost Craver Marvel, which was named after Army Reservist Alan Craver who, during a deployment as a water purification specialist, saved a contingent of the 10th Mountain Division when he manned a Barret M107 .50 caliber rifle and gave covering fire while the team was ambushed approaching the COP. During the ambush, Craver successfully covered the team and refused to take shelter himself until they were safely inside the COP. He was eventually killed by enemy fire.

The COP was nothing to look at. It was a converted lumberyard that had served as an operating base for U.S. and British forces for nearly ten years. It mostly consisted of a system of mazes of rock and sandbag barricades with watch posts and terraces carved into the western hillside. The south side of the base was designated as the landing zone for supply helicopters and gunships. The northern and eastern perspectives gave a clear killing zone of a full kilometer, and access to the Pech River and adjacent roads that connected the mountain villages. The buildings were mostly plywood with some stone reinforcement and bunkers. The command post itself was dug into the hillside and contained a communications and planning area with its own generator and ventilation system.

The Second Platoon of the SEAL Troop flew the 170 kilometers from Bagram to the COP in a Chinook CH-47 helicopter escorted by two Apache gunships. The trip took less than an hour by air. By roads, what there were of them, the trip would take two days. If the Troop was in enemy contact, they could have air support within forty minutes of the initial contact notification. Speed was generally on the side of the ISAF but stealth and surprise were on the side of the Taliban.

The trip from Bagram to the COP was uneventful. As they unloaded their own supplies along with replenishments for the other support troops still at the COP, Doc Burk could not help but comment on the amenities—or lack of them.

"Can anyone tell me what the U.S. Navy is doing in the mountains of a landlocked country?"

"Take it easy, Eeyore! This is a beautiful spot," Boomer shot back. "I can't wait to schedule my first spa treatment."

"Not so quick, Boomer," Todd said. "We have 0800 tee times tomorrow."

The joking around continued as the rest of the team joined in and they offloaded equipment.

Todd took Zip to an area that served as a makeshift kennel

when other military working dogs were present and left him there until he could get everything else settled. Zip paced back and forth in the large pen, trying to get used to all the new sights and smells. He wasn't comfortable in this place and it was going to take some time to settle in. Later when Todd and the team got their billeting assignments and were able to get the quarters established, Todd came back for Zip. The COP was set up such that there were no common sleeping areas, so Zip and Todd actually had their own small, eight-by-eight quarters. It was tight but comfortable. That night both Todd and Zip slept uncomfortably and Zip was up listening and sniffing around for most of the night.

It took a few days for Zip to settle down. Todd let him loose on his own before they got into their racks. This way Zip could do his own patrol of the grounds and make sure everything was secure before returning to quarters. When he did his checks, he noted the smells of the night and how the lights from the villages and other lights around the COP looked. He mapped these in his head so that he could quickly assess when things were out of the ordinary.

Lieutenant Kelly was busy doing the same thing as he watched Zip make his rounds. However, Kelly took greater measures in his evaluations. He diligently studied radio surveillance reports and drone reconnaissance photographs, examining the photos for any small changes. He tried to note the positions of rock formations, vehicle parking, and the debris piles around the villages. Even a small change could indicate the placement of IEDs. His team was preparing for their first incursions to the local villages and he didn't want any surprises.

Lieutenant Kelly worked out a system for moving from village to village in a manner that would allow him to assess reconnaissance reports before and after the incursions, in order to continually evaluate apparent changes in the routines of each village. Their first stop was the village of Ashat—a remarkably unremarkable little speck of houses, goats, and terraced fields carved into the hillside. The village was one of those that exist off the many capillary valleys of the larger Pech River Valley. The people of the village were part of the Pathan Tribe, and legend had it that the Pathans were actually the lost tribe of Israel who were long ago converted to Islam.

The team cautiously made their way into the town and Abby made arrangements to speak to the Shuras, or local tribal council.

Abby introduced the senior members of the SEAL Team to the Shuras, and explained that they were there to see to any of their needs including medicine, building materials, or agricultural tools. The goal was to convince the Shuras that their mission was not one of conquest, but of support to ensure they had what they needed to thrive as an independent village and as a tribe. The tactic was largely successful as long as they could maintain a small level of trust and the Shuras believed they were not aggressors or concealing secondary motives.

While Abby, Lieutenant Kelly, and Penman met with the Shuras, the rest of the squad set up a defensive perimeter. Todd and Zip took a "walk" to let Zip sniff around the village. Their job was to check for weapons and explosives without actually looking like they were checking for weapons and explosives. It was all part of the trust game, made more difficult by the fact that *everyone* in the Hindu Kush was armed. Todd and Zip needed to differentiate between being armed defensively and stockpiling caches of arms to be used offensively. This took a balance of professional and political experience and intuition.

If the meeting with the Shuras was somehow strained and the appearance and actions of the villagers were too distant or too cordial, the proverbial red flags would go up. This particular meeting was going fine. The meeting with the tribal council was not rushed, and they were requesting some tools to help improve irrigation of their terraced fields. Lieutenant Kelly assured them he would arrange for a team of engineers to visit the village and supply the equipment and instruction. Outside, most of the villagers were indifferent to what was going on. They had been through this before and knew how the game was played. The children were interested in Zip but knew they were never to approach a military animal, so they spent their time kicking balls and tagging along behind the other members of the squad.

Their first few visits to the villages followed this same routine for the most part. The SEAL Team and Abby were able to work with the various tribal councils and help with their assorted needs. Several times, Doc Burk treated some of the villagers with medical issues, mostly providing antibiotics for small infections or other minor treatments. As March turned into April and the weather steadily improved, activity around the area began to intensify. Most of it was just the normal goings-on of a rural society emerging from winter to spring—but it was also a time for the team to be on a higher level of awareness. The more general movements happened, the more nefarious movements could be hidden.

The team first encountered this on their way to visit another small village called Darbat. They were moving up the road with a ravine on the left side and a hillside on the right in two armored Humvees. As they made their way around the corner of the hill, Lieutenant Kelly noticed a burned-out Toyota pickup truck on the side of the road. At the same time, Zip snapped to attention and Kelly ordered the two Humvees to stop. Zip stood frozen, staring intently at the shell of the truck, and Todd knew something was up. Kelly's voice came over Todd's communication headset.

"Mitchell."

"Yes sir."

"You see the truck, right?"

"Yes, and it has Zip's interest too."

"Alright, I want the team out in a fifty-meter spread. Hancock, stay on the M240 in the forward Humvee while Mitchell and Zip check this thing out. Angel, take a position up the slope and let us know what is moving out there." Kelly's orders were clear and the team moved quietly and efficiently. "OK Mitchell. Nice and slow. Let's see what we have."

Todd checked Zip's Kevlar flak jacket and then his own. He then looked up at Radar manning the machine gun in the turret of the Humvee.

"Are we good, Mike?" Todd said.

"Clear."

"Angel, how we looking?"

"Clear."

Zip and Todd dismounted and descended into the shallow part of the ravine so that they could stay beneath the blast if one was to come. If there *was* an IED it could be triggered remotely from as far away as a quarter mile. For this reason, all eyes of the team were scanning away from the truck. When they were about twenty meters from the truck, Todd rolled up onto the road and Zip came to his side, keeping his chest low to the ground as he had been trained to do. As they positioned themselves on the road, Zip halted immediately and focused his gaze at the base of the truck. This was the indication that he smelled components of an explosive device and was signaling danger.

"Hold it," Todd said calmly through his comms set. "Zip has something."

The team remained motionless but they all took note. They were still scanning the area to see if there might be anyone watching and waiting to press a button remotely, but there was no sign of anything unusual. Zip and Todd remained motionless on the road for another minute and Todd slowly pulled out his targeting optic scope from the side pocket of his battle dress pants to get a closer look. He peered through the scope at the base of the truck but could not make out anything that looked like a device. He looked to the other side of the road where there was another small pile of metal debris. Although he couldn't see it, he was convinced by Zip's actions that there was something present. Todd scanned back and forth from the shell of the truck to the other side of the road. He pushed the laser sighting on the scope and, as he made passes back and forth and up and down, something glimmered. He checked again, and as he moved the light, the glimmer continued in a straight line from one side of the road to the other, the laser reflecting from the object.

"Lieutenant Kelly, there's a trip wire across the road. It looks like it's about five meters in front of the truck, probably on a short delay. Do you want me to take a closer look?"

"Negative," Kelly said. "There's no one here. Let's get Sugar out and trip it from a distance."

"Affirmative," Todd acknowledged.

The team regrouped and redeployed to form a new perimeter moving the Humvees back another fifty meters while R.J. and Todd unpacked and quickly assembled a compact remote-controlled robot. It looked a little like a small-tracked vehicle but also had a telescopic arm with a pair of pincers on the end and a point-of-view optical sight that could be seen from a screen held by the operator. The SUGV 310 was nicknamed "Sugar" by the team. While R.J. operated the robot, Todd replaced Radar in the Humvee turret and directed R.J. to the wire.

"OK Senior Chief, take it right up the middle of the road," Todd said as he watched the robot approach the wire through his binoculars. "Another two meters and you're there. OK, stop! Now raise the arm up about a meter and come forward just a bit."

R. J. did as directed and brought the arm of the robot to just above the wire. "Looks good, R.J. Fire in the hole," Todd calmly informed the squad, and they all tucked and turned away from the projected blast area, ensuring they had adequate cover. Todd moved Zip down under the back seat of the Humvee.

"Do it, R.J."

And with that, the robot arm dropped, breaking the trip wire. Nothing happened.

"Wait for it …," Todd said.

Three seconds went by before the concussion of an exploding 152 mm Russian artillery shell shook the ground and echoed down the valley. The blast, which was directed from the truck debris across the road into the hillside making a hole a full meter in diameter, would have cut through any layer of armor on the Humvees.

"Holy Shit!" Boomer exclaimed. "Somebody around here really doesn't like us."

"Quiet!" Kelly said. "Angel, do you see anything?"

"Negative. Just dust."

"Alright, let's check the road near the truck and get moving. Fox, move up the road another hundred meters and check around the bend. We should have a straight shot into Darbat from there."

Fox took the point and started to move up the road and around the bend of the hillside. Just then, Zip scrambled out of the open door of the back seat of the Humvee and sprinted up the road toward Fox. Todd didn't notice at first since he and R.J. were busy assessing Sugar for damage. Zip shot past Todd and galloped toward where Fox was walking. About ten meters from Fox, he skidded to a stop and let out a series of high-pitched barks.

Todd looked up at the sound of Zip's bark and knew something was wrong. "Jim, don't move," he said through his comm set.

Fox stopped in his tracks and froze where he was. Zip was spinning in a circle, trying to get his attention. It looked as though he wanted to go to Fox, but couldn't advance.

"Jim, don't turn around. Start walking backwards towards us retracing your exact steps." Todd instructed. "Angel will guide you."

Nakamura trained his sights on Fox and spotted him back to the squad, step by step.

When Fox got back he said, "What was that all about?"

"Look at Zip," Todd said, "he's going nuts. Something else is out there."

Kelly knew it right away. "They mined the road too," he said into his comm set. "If they didn't get us with the IED, they wanted us to relax a little and hope that we'd hit the mines. They were almost right. Get the Humvees to the side of the road and wire them. We go in on foot from here."

The team took a number of breaching charges and booby trapped the Humvees to "discourage" anyone from tampering with the vehicles. Kelly radioed the COP and informed them of the situation and arranged for the mines to be identified and removed. Then the SEAL team hiked the remaining two kilometers into the village of Darbat, with Todd and Zip on point.

When they reached the outskirts of the village they were greeted by two of the Shuras who welcomed them in and asked if they were all in good health. They had heard the explosion, they said, and were concerned that everyone was alright. They seemed a little too welcoming, and it only served to intensify the mood. Abby, Lieutenant Kelly, and Penman started up their normal dialogue with the Shuras, who assured them that they had seen nothing over the last couple of weeks. During the winter, they had been visited by one group of Taliban insurgents, but only briefly, and they asked only for food as they moved through the valley, and the villagers only fed them because Zakat, the Islamic pillar of aid and alms giving, required them to do so.

They talked for another thirty minutes and the Shuras continually reassured Kelly that they were not in need of anything and had no loyalties to the Taliban. Outside, the situation told a different story. Some of the buildings were in an advanced state of disrepair and the agricultural terraces were beginning to collapse. They would never hold the water of the spring rains. Abby looked at Lieutenant Kelly and subtly shook his head. The village had been compromised.

Lieutenant Kelly ordered the team to conduct a search of the village. They had been attacked and lied to, and it was time for a more direct approach. The team unslung their weapons and moved systematically from building to building. Abby politely insisted that the Shuras remain in the house where they had just talked, stationing Radar and Fox outside. Todd, Boomer, and Zip moved into each hut, allowing Zip time to check each corner and catch a scent. Doc Burk and R.J. covered each entry and Angel covered the approaching road. While the searches progressed, Abby and

Penman interviewed each of the villagers. All of them had the same story about the winter visit by the Taliban and that the stop was largely uneventful. The consistency of their stories was another indication that there was something amiss. No three people ever told the same version of a story, let alone a village of one hundred. Despite all the warning signs, however, Todd, Boomer, and Zip found nothing. Finally, it was getting to be late afternoon and Kelly had no desire to have his team making its way back to the COP after dark. He called them back together.

"There's definitely something wrong here but we can't stay. Whoever left that last surprise might be rigging something for us on our way back and I'll be damned if I want to make that trip in the dark."

"Hooyah, Sir!" Stock replied. "This place is creepy. Everyone here looks like a zombie."

"Alright, let's get moving."

As they packed up their equipment and prepared to leave, a breeze started up and traveled down the valley. With it came a scent that caught Zip's attention. He perked up his ears and stuck his nose into the air to evaluate the smell.

"Hang on a second, Lieutenant. Take a look at Zip."

"What's he got?"

"I'm not sure, but he seems to have picked up something coming down off the terraces."

"You have five minutes. Check it out. I want eyes on those buildings and Angel and Fox on the second level of terraces. Move, and make it clear that we want to be left alone!"

The team quickly did as they were told and Todd, Boomer, and Zip moved up toward the first level of terraces; the ones that looked dilapidated. As they got closer to the first set, Zip snapped rigid and fixed on the base of the terrace.

"He definitely has something here," Todd remarked.

"Look. There's fresh dirt under the left terrace," Boomer said.

"I see it. Let's take a closer look."

The three deliberately approached the terrace, scanning for mines and booby traps. When they reached the soft dirt, Todd delicately poked into it with his field knife and hit something hard. He then carefully removed the top layer of soil to reveal a trap door. Todd took off his gloves and moved his fingers around the seam of the door to determine if there was anything dangerous around the hinges.

"Lieutenant Kelly, I don't feel anything here. It doesn't appear to be wired and there's just a normal padlock on this door. It looks like this was all put here in a big hurry and they didn't have time to booby trap it. I can get in easily by taking off the hinges. Boomer, take Zip back to the squad."

Kelly gave the go ahead and Todd pulled out the electric screwdriver he used to service Sugar. The door was just plywood and the screws came out easily. He alternated loosening screws, one at a time on the top and bottom hinge, until he could be remove them with his fingers. When the last screw was out, he wedged a piece of wood under the door so it wouldn't fall off the frame. Then he carefully moved the door about a half-inch off the hinge and again looked along all the seams and peeked behind the door with his flashlight. There was no sign of anything dangerous in the door, so he moved it a foot off the frame to get a full view of what was behind it. When his flashlight hit the contents of the hollowed out space beneath the terrace, he whistled long and low.

"Lieutenant Kelly, I don't know what these guys were telling you but I don't think it was the truth." Todd fully removed the door while Kelly came up to take a look.

"We're going to need some help with this," Kelly said after he pulled his head out of the shaft.

Inside the makeshift cave was a stash of RPG-7 rocket launchers, AK 47 assault rifles, PMN antipersonnel mines, 82 mm mortar rounds and about three dozen 152 mm artillery shells like the one rigged in the IED intended for the team. There was enough weaponry and ammunition to support fifty troops.

Kelly radioed what they had found and requested relief and troop replacement by helicopter. The team secured the area and the cache of weapons, and waited for the reinforcements to arrive. Kelly then radioed for a British SAS Team to meet them near the Humvees, to provide support for their return to the COP. There was no way he was taking the team back out there, alone.

###

A mile away, smartly concealed among the rocks and brush in such a way that would have impressed even POFC Nakamura, Tajwah Rabbani muttered a Pashto curse under his breath. The Americans had ruined a full six months of stockpiling, and their plans could now be in jeopardy if any one of those sheep in the village opened his mouth too much. He knew he could not stay where he was because he could see through his binoculars that the short one was already on the radio, telling what they had found. No doubt helicopter gunship and troop support was on the way. Within the hour, the whole portion of this valley would be full of American and British soldiers.

When he could hear the echo of helicopter rotors bouncing off the mountains into the valley, Tajwah Rabbani used the cover of the sound and the setting sun to disappear into the hills.

Chapter 9
Stronger Than My Enemies

When the helicopters arrived, Lieutenant Kelly briefed the engineers and relief troops on the situation. He left Abby and Penman to assist with the interrogation of the locals while he gathered the rest of his squad and returned to the Humvees. When they got back to the vehicles, an additional squad of British SAS personnel was making its way up the road in a couple of FV432 Bulldog Armored Personnel Carriers to escort the team back to the COP. The Brits reported that their trip was uneventful and they expected a smooth ride back to the COP.

As Abby, Penman, and two Naval Intelligence Officers who had accompanied the engineers interviewed the Shuras, the truth of the situation began to come out. The Taliban had been in and out of the village for the past three months moving equipment and people through the hills. Darbat had become a resting stop between where they were coming and going. They estimated about 200 men had been through the area carrying weapons and ammunition. The Taliban had appropriated nearly all of their winter stores and assured them they would be well taken care of in the spring but no further help ever arrived. Toward the end of the winter, they began leaving arms at the village and, when they heard that the ISAF was stepping up their incursions to the local villages, they hastily dug the storage area that the team discovered.

The Taliban had held the villagers in a constant state of fear and false hope. They took the tribal elder's granddaughters and grandson away, promising their safe return if the villagers continued to cooperate. When the SEALs found the weapons and ammunition, all hope evaporated. As Abby and Penman interviewed the elder, he broke down and began to sob. He told them that since the village had failed to protect the weapons, his grandchildren were all but dead. The village would be marked and when the Taliban returned, Darbat would cease to exist.

The Intelligence Team assured the elders otherwise. They told them that food and supplies were on the way. They were arranging for a platoon of Green Berets to come and assist them with training the remaining men of the village to use the weapons left by the Taliban. They would set up a system of communication the elders could use to call for help if needed. Also, they would arrange for increased meetings with the neighboring villages to form a coalition to help each other share resources.

The Shuras were not placated. They had seen this routine before. The Taliban were like cockroaches—one could come in and stifle them for a time but they would always come back. Someday the soldiers would be gone but the fanatics would still be there, waiting for the next opportunity.

Abby tried to explain his situation to them and his belief that, if they banded together and remained strong with the help of the military, they could push the Taliban out. The Shuras looked at Abby and coldly responded, "We are talking to a dead man."

Abby sighed and said to Penman, "These people are beaten. Their spirit is broken and they are now just part of the landscape. I don't think we can do anything here."

Penman was a little more optimistic. "It looks bad Abby but let's see what the engineers and Green Berets can do. They'll get the Shuras from the next village over here and try to be the diplomats in all of this."

"I hope you are right, my friend."

###

Ten kilometers away, Tajwah Rabbani was returning to the

camp of Mullah Nur Mohammed Karmal. The Taliban had developed an ingenious system of caves and various encampments within the Hindu Kush Mountains and Korengal Valley that had helped repel invaders for centuries. This particular camp included a system of caves and tunnels that went on for several kilometers in the mountains, opening into a small network of pastures that were used for grazing livestock. Nur Mohammed Karmal knew every inch of this territory. His brilliant use of both ruthless and sometimes humanitarian tactics, intimidation, and concealment had made him a formidable enemy. Karmal was almost a legend; seemingly more myth than actual person. There was only one known photograph of the man, and that was disputed. Even his personal history was a mystery. The villagers told stories that he was a direct descendent of the Prophet Mohammad. He was said to be "God's Warrior" and impervious to harm by the infidel. The truth was something completely different.

Nur Mohammad Karmal was indeed a mere mortal. He was orphaned when his parents were killed by Pakistani military police during a demonstration, and placed under the care of his maternal uncle along the Pakistan-Afghanistan border. Karmal's uncle was an extremist who despised the ways of the West and instilled that hate in his nephew. The uncle made sure to poison the mind of his nephew as he began to manufacture a man of hate. Karmal's education was a mixture of half-truths and complete lies about the infidels and their crusades and attempted corruption of Islam and the teachings of the Prophet. Karmal was taught the Koran, but only those passages that emphasized the need to protect the word and punish the transgressor. When Karmal's uncle sent him away to the Darul Uloom Haqqania Madrassa in Akora Khattak, Pakistan, at the age of thirteen, he handed over the essence of an extremist.

The Imams of the madrassa began to mold the clay of hate into the personality of a fanatic. They taught him to speak and become a talented orator. They were impressed by this child's ability to easily memorize the Koran and to recite the passages with conviction. They taught him to listen; to take the thoughts of others, repackage them, and twist them into his own agenda. There was brilliance of the worst kind in this child. A world of hardship, oppression, religious extremism, and political manipulation had created a dangerous human being who could be used as an effective weapon against those the Imams saw as a threat.

The Imams were successful at manufacturing their religious zealot, but the child needed to learn the ways of destruction. For this, he was sent to learn from Al-Qaeda's Lashkar Al Zil or "The Shadow Army." The Lashkar Al Zil was a paramilitary unit consisting of the reformed 055 Brigade which was the Taliban's Special Forces. It included many former Mujahideen. Karmal learned the craft of war by being a direct aid to commander Abdullah Said Al Libi. When he joined the Shadow Army in the early '90s he also met a man who would become his mentor for a brief time. Ali Mohamed was a double agent. He was closely tied to Al-Qaeda, but also acted as an advisor to the U.S. Coalition. He trained with the U.S. Special Forces at Ft. Bragg and taught Karmal about the U.S. Military structure and tactics during his time in Afghanistan. The lessons Karmal learned from Al Libi and Ali Mohamed shaped him into an efficient weapon.

Karmal developed charisma by studying the great religious, military, and political leaders. He was especially imbued with the exploits of Sheik Omar Abdel-Rahman also known as the "Blind Sheik." Abdel-Rahman had been convicted of organizing the first World Trade Center bombing and was the inspiration for the more insidious attacks perpetrated by Osama bin Laden. Ali Mohamed knew the Blind Sheik and spoke of him as if he were a mystic. Mohamed would later be caught and convicted of conspiracy for his part in plots to bomb embassies in Kenya and Tanzania.

Because of Mohamed's stories about the Blind Sheik and a desire to keep a sense of mystery about himself, Karmal took to always wearing dark glasses so that no one could look into his eyes and possibly secure a glimpse into his empty soul.

Now, as he stood at the edge of a shallow crevasse and watched Rabbani approach the camp, Karmal could see the dejection on Rabbani's face and knew that it would not be good news. He pushed the heavy glasses up on the bridge of his long nose and resolved to steel himself to whatever the news was to be. He listened to Rabbani give his report about the SEAL Team incursion and discovery of the weapons cache then told Rabbani that he was thankful for his safe return and instructed him to rest and get some food. He would organize a meeting of his commanders in two hours so that Rabanni could deliver his report again to the entire group. Karmal was an expert at managing a meeting.

His commanders were a small and close-knit group who had been operating in the mountains of the Hindu Kush for most of their adult lives. Karmal's approach was to frame a discussion, then take a knee in the middle of the group and let them opine. Sometimes he would let the conversation go on for hours without saying a word. This was the case for the current situation. His advisors listened to Rabbani's report and discussed options. Some of them suggested returning to Darbat and wiping it off the map as they had done to other villages that had defied or disappointed them. Others suggested they send suicide bombers to the COP. Karmal patiently listened and said nothing. Eventually, when the discussion deteriorated into a circular argument and Karmal knew that his group had explored all options, it was time for him to intercede and make decisions.

As was his custom, he rose from the middle of the group and stepped to an area of the room that allowed whatever light source was available to hit him in a particular manner that illuminated him but still kept a portion in the shadows. When he addressed any group, his first words were always a softly spoken. *As-salāmu ʿalaykumā*, "Peace be upon you."

"My brothers," he began. "Thank you for the useful discussion. Allah has blessed me with talented leaders and advisors. We are facing another group of formidable enemies but their arrogance will once again bring their demise. They think they have crippled us and are now gathering further intelligence from the people of Darbat and formulating their next steps against us. We must keep them off balance.

"Tajwah, I must once again ask you to be the tip of my sword."

Tajwah Rabbani nodded in reverent compliance.

"The Americans think they have won a victory, when in fact they have only scored a point. They will be itching for more. Tajwah will take three men to their nest and poke at them until they are angry enough to swarm. When they do, he and his men will lead them away to the ruins near Bebiyal.

"Tajwah, you must make a retreat that looks as though a professional soldier is trying to mask an escape. But don't conceal too much. We want the Americans to believe they are being clever in their ability to track you. When you arrive at the ruins, dig yourselves in and wait for us. There will be food, water, and additional arms waiting for you. We will not be far. Bebiyal is a perfect spot for us. It is in a place that tapers into a narrow valley. Their helicopter air support will be ineffective."

"Teacher;" Abdur Rahman spoke. Rahman was Karmal's explosive expert and an especially cruel man. "What of those sheep in Darbat? They betray us at this very moment."

"What exactly do they know, Abdur?" Karmal replied, nearly dismissing the comment and question. "We will soon pay them another visit and educate them on the consequences of impiety. For now, we will deal with that elder's grandchildren. Send the boy to our brothers at the madrassa in Akora Khattak that he might come to know Allah and someday rejoin us in Jihad. Send the girls back to Darbat—" He paused and looked slowly around the circle at his commanders. "But only the heads. We will keep the rest as retribution for Darbat's imprudence."

Chapter 10
If Knocked Down, I Will Get Back Up, Every Time

The mood at COP Craver Marvel was relaxed and the members of the squad were feeling pretty good about themselves. They had done their job and avoided casualties and did not even have to fire a round. It was the kind of incursion that the SEALs liked. None of them was the stereotypical, combat-hungry warrior portrayed in the movies. It was fine with them that their work had been done with a complete absence of drama. They all understood that this probably would not remain the case.

It had been three days since Abby and Penman returned from Darbat. Despite what Karmal thought about the villagers of Darbat, they were quite perceptive and noticed much more than the men of Karmal's forces realized. Abby and Penman learned the names of some of the men who had passed through the village, as well as specifics about their clothing and weapons. Lieutenant Kelly was reviewing the information with Naval Intelligence and passing it through the CIA database. Abby was sure he had heard some of those names during his time in the Korengal Valley, and some of them were associated with the Taliban leader who for now was known only as "God's Warrior."

The Green Berets were still at the village when the remains of the tribal elder's granddaughters were returned. The horror of Karmal's intimidation tactic had the opposite effect of what he expected. Instead of instilling more fear and subservience in the people of Darbat, it galvanized them in their hatred of the Taliban. The Green Berets were experts at tribal relations, and were successful at bringing together the people of Ashat and Darbat to begin working together. They fed the village and were able to create an alliance between them. Karmal had miscalculated.

After a debriefing at the COP, the squad was able to stand down a bit and relax. They brought in some steaks, shrimp, and sausage and even managed to smuggle in a couple cases of beer. Boomer made a giant batch of Lowcountry boil, which the British SAS soldiers had never tasted. They became giant fans of southern cooking after that evening and contributed a couple bottles of good single malt Scotch whisky to the festivities. Later, everyone went to hang out in small groups or spend time alone.

Boomer retired to his rack to binge-watch *Breaking Bad* while most of the rest of the squad started a Texas Hold'em tournament. They were all hoping that Doc Burk would abstain since he was widely recognized as the best poker player at the Norfolk Navy Station, if not the entire Navy. They weren't so lucky. Doc joined the game and patiently picked the other players apart until the entire stack of chips sat in front of him.

Todd was able to get off a couple emails back to Pennsylvania to let everyone know he was doing fine and missing them all. He took some time to himself, sitting outside with Zip and enjoying the cool air and gentle breeze of the evening. He sat in a beach chair with Zip by his side and threw a tennis ball against the side of the COP mud and stone wall. Zip caught it each time it came off the wall and dutifully dropped it by the side of the chair. Todd was lost in thought, mindlessly bouncing the ball off the wall, when Abby sidled next to him with his eyes downcast, uncharacteristically demure.

"Petty Officer Mitchell," Abby began, "may I speak with you?"

Todd bounced the ball off the wall one last time and as Zip caught it, Todd began to direct him away so that he would not be close to Abby during their conversation, in accordance with their agreement.

Abby raised his hand to stop Todd. "Petty Officer, that won't be necessary. In fact, this is part of what I would like to talk to you about."

Todd, surprised at this turn, shrugged his shoulders and stopped Zip from moving away, signaling him to come instead. Zip plopped down beside him and occupied himself by chewing on the tennis ball.

"Mr. Mitchell, I believe I have misjudged you and Zip," Abby said. This was the first time he had actually used Zip's name. "I have never seen an animal perform in such a way as he did the other day at Darbat. He most likely saved Mr. Fox's life and allowed us to find those weapons. This is truly a special animal." Abby remained standing at parade rest with his hands behind his back. If he was going to humble himself and admit he was wrong, he was going to do it standing and in a dignified posture.

"Thank you, Abby. He is special and he is one of the team. This is what I've been working for. I've given him more privilege and included him in everything the squad does so that he knows us as his family. He does what he does not only because of his training, but because of the special loyalty and bond that we all feel as brothers in the SEALs. He is not a piece of equipment. He is a U.S. Navy SEAL as much as any one of us who survived BUD/S training. Now, the Navy may not agree with me on this but all of us in the squad understand. And I appreciate your sentiment."

"Thank you. May I call you Todd?"

"Of course."

"Todd, as I misjudged you and Zip, I feel you may misjudge me, too. I know you have prejudice against Muslims and I can see the disgust on your face when you observe what we can do to each other and to outsiders—but this is not the way of Islam. At least not the Islam I was taught. My reading of the Koran has influenced a tolerance for all people. My family has always had a profound sense of charity as one of our primary tenets. We have seen that, for centuries, the Middle East was a center for science, architecture, medicine, government and law that influence even modern Western society. This is the Islam I dream of—a world where I am permitted to educate my daughters where they might achieve all their potential. I wish we could have civil discourse among all tribes and governments and put an end to the butchering. I fear I will never see this.

"You see, my options are limited. I watched the men play your poker game tonight and, although I am forbidden to gamble, I see that I am "all in" as they say during the game. If we are not successful here, the Taliban will hunt me down. They will hunt down my wife and children. I will no doubt be tortured and eventually lose my head. What they will do to my girls, I do not wish to even imagine."

"Abby," Todd politely interrupted, "Why are you telling me all this?"

"I have repeatedly applied for asylum for my family in the U.S. with the hopes that my wife and daughters might live in safety. I have already spoken to Scott about this and explained my situation but I want to explain myself to you, also. The bureaucracy of the situation is maddening. I understand your father is an attorney." Abby paused, reluctant to beg a favor, forcing his pride into parade rest, too. "I do not ask of this for myself. I am willing to stay here and die for my cause if that is Allah's will."

"Abby, I don't know what I can do for you. If you haven't noticed, I am not the best politician and I am certainly not one of Lieutenant Kelly's favorites."

"You sell yourself short, Petty Officer. I feel you are one of the most respected people here, even if they are sometimes angry with you. They follow your actions and always listen to what you have to say, even Lieutenant Kelly."

"I appreciate that Abby. I'll see if we can help when I contact home again, but I can't make any promises."

"That is all I can ask," Abby said. Then he reached down and petted Zip for the first time.

The temperature had dropped a few degrees and the wind slightly shifted. As Abby withdrew has fingers from Zip's soft ears and rough mane, Zip suddenly snapped to attention and the black zigzag of fur on his back stood straight up. He jumped up on the edge of the compound wall and peered deep into the darkness, concentrating on something over on the other side of the helicopter landing zone. The muscles in his shoulders contracted and his tail and ears shot erect.

"Are we expecting anyone?" Todd said, trying to draw a bead on what Zip was staring at.

"I don't know," Abby said as he also looked out across the

field.

The three stood motionless and peered into the night, looking for any sign of movement. Then, they saw it—a brief flash of light followed by a muffled thud.

"Down!" Todd yelled loud enough to be heard throughout the COP. "Zip, down!" he yelled again. Zip jumped off the wall, taking cover next to the compound structure.

Before Todd could get out another warning cry, the first explosion hit the top of the command bunker and was followed by two more mortar rounds of high explosive—one falling harmlessly right outside the front gate of the COP, but the second landing squarely on the living quarters. Within seconds of the third explosion, the British SAS sentry opened fire into the darkness towards the direction of the flash with his L1A1 .50 caliber heavy machine gun. Every third round, coated with phosphorus, glowed in the night. He guided the tracer rounds into the area of the flash and ran off another two hundred before stopping to check if there was any further activity.

As the echoes of the explosions and machine gun fire dissipated through the valley, Fox picked his head up to survey the damage.

"Boomer!" he cried as he gaped at the pile of debris that was once the squad's living quarters.

Within seconds, fifteen men and one dog began to dig frantically through the wreckage, desperate to get to their friend. They hurled pieces of the structure aside and yelled for Boomer while they drove through the mess. Zip dug at the pile with the rest of the team, but he didn't know exactly what they were looking for. He was overwhelmed with the smells of explosive residue, scorched plastic, and smoldering wood. The smells of the personal effects of every man on the team floated everywhere. After two minutes, they paused and yelled again. No response.

As they resumed the search with critical urgency, ten feet away from where they shoveled a massive fist punched through a cracked piece of plywood. Then, slowly, the heap of rubble shifted as the giant form of Boomer Stock emerged dressed only in boxer shorts.

"Dammit!" he said as he brushed the dirt and blood off his body. "Just when Walt was daring Jessie to shoot him." Banged up but walking, it was typical Boomer—lightening the mood.

Doc Burk rushed up to him and examined Boomer for further

trauma beyond the many visible cuts and scratches.

"I'm fine Doc, those assholes can't hurt me. I'm like Wolverine. I heal right up again."

"OK, Wolverine," Doc Burk deadpanned. "Let's get your butt to the infirmary and make sure."

As the two walked off with Boomer straight as an arrow, unwilling to show the pain on his face, something caught Zip's attention and he went back to work digging in the pile. The team watched him in silence as he burrowed with renewed determination like a terrier trying to ferret a rodent out of its hole. Todd wondered if they had missed someone but all the Brits and SEALs were accounted for. Soon, only Zip's tail was visible, standing straight out. Then it began to wag as Zip backed out of the hole, his Frisbee in his mouth and a proud look on his face.

"Well, at least he has his priorities straight," Angel chuckled.

As Zip shook off the dirt, Lieutenant Kelly emerged and commenced getting the team focused on the situation at hand.

"OK, let's get a survey of the damage and see what we've lost. Radar, I want you and Angel to check the whole place and see what defenses may have been breached. Fox and Penman, start sorting through this mess and see what personal effects and bunks we can salvage. We'll set up living arrangements in the infirmary and CP, for the time being. R.J.—"

"Yes, Sir?"

"Take Abby, Mitchell, and Zip and coordinate with the Brits. Let's get a little recon done and see if our visitors left anything."

As the team moved into action, Kelly stopped R.J. and called him back to discuss what had happened.

"What do you think, Senior Chief?"

"I think we were lucky L.T.," R.J. answered. "I also think we touched a nerve when we found those Tali party supplies back at Darbat. They were here for a little payback and their aim was pretty good. They got off three rounds of H.E. in pretty short order and I'll bet our patrols find no trace. I also think they'll be back. That was easy for them and they'll think they can do it again."

"Thank you R.J.," Kelly said, acknowledging his opinion and dismissing the Sr. Chief to rejoin the patrol.

Lieutenant Kelly reflected on what R.J. had said and set about making a plan to deal with a potential return. He balanced the unknowns in his head. What was the meaning of the attack and what would be the next best course of action? He saw it in one of three ways, the first of which agreed with R.J.'s observations. This attack was simply revenge for finding the weapons. They'd do hit-and-runs and harass with no strategy other than to continually weaken the camp and prohibit them from ever relaxing. The second possibility was that this was a probing attack. They were checking the camp's defenses to see what they were up against so they could prepare a larger attack with vehicles or suicide squads.

The last possibility was a taunting. They wanted the Americans to come after them, like a base runner daring the pitcher to try and pick him off. If this was the case, Kelly was tempted to take the bait. The upside was that they could capture a few of them and gain some valuable intelligence against this mysterious Mullah that the tribes feared so much. He would discuss all of this with Intelligence and Commander Heard back at Bagram to decide next steps.

Chapter 11
The Trust of Those I Have Sworn to Protect

Lieutenant Kelly contacted the SEAL command team back at Bagram to debrief them on the attack and discuss what it might mean. The opinion of command was that the Taliban had made a mistake and had exposed themselves. They saw this as an opportunity to shift the balance and go on the offensive. Also, since time was not on their side anymore, they could not afford to continue to make altogether conservative moves. The drawdown was in full swing and there would be fewer and fewer combat troops in Afghanistan to fully confront the Taliban. Lieutenant Kelly's orders were that, if and when the Taliban attempted another attack, he was to have his team ready to pursue. Commander Heard agreed with Kelly's opinion that there was an opportunity to acquire a prisoner or two and gather additional intelligence on this mysterious warrior in the mountains.

The next day, Kelly had his team make a full survey of the COP, tactically examining every area around the COP that might be advantageous for a Tali mortar attack. The team came back with what amounted to five options that, allowing for range and trajectory, might cause the most damage to the COP and still leave an avenue of escape. They used the remaining daylight to establish intrusion warning devices and line-of-sight night vision. When the Taliban made another attempt on the COP, the SEALs would be ready to pounce.

###

Cleverly concealed in the hills outside the COP, Tajwah Rabbani silently watched the SEALs conduct their survey and made mental notes of their activities. He would let the Americans set their traps, and wait an additional night before making another attack. If he waited, they might think that the previous bombardment was a onetime event and relax their defenses a bit. Anyway, tarrying for another night would allow for a new moon and give him and his three colleagues the much-needed added darkness to make their retreat and lure the Americans from their holes for the chase.

###

That night there were no barbeques or card games at COP Craver Marvel. The entire group was on alert with surveillance set up at the five identified points. Todd and Zip were overseeing the spot where the first attack occurred. Both of them were equipped with night vision equipment. Zip's was a specially designed K9 version that gave him exceptional depth of vision but blocked out all peripheral sight. He still struggled with the discipline needed to wear the uncomfortable goggles and not push them off his head since they essentially eliminated his normal 270-degree field of vision. The night was exceptionally quiet with a constant wind prevailing through the valley from west to east. A couple of times throughout the night, Zip caught fleeting scents in the air and rose to attention to see if he could identify anything, but as soon as a scent would come, it would be gone again. Near dawn, they were both relieved of their post and retired to the CP for a few hours rest before being sent on patrol again outside the COP.

###

Rabbani watched the SEALs again the next day. He had picked his area of attack. It was one that gave him the least advantage on angle for the mortar barrage, but one that he felt he could reach without detection. It also gave him two options for escape through the mountain pass, and a near-direct route to the Bebiyal ruins where Karmal would be waiting to slaughter the infidel crusaders.

At dusk, he took advantage of the shifting shadows against the valley walls to move into position as the sun fell below the horizon.

Rabbani took up his position with the brothers Abdul and Nadir Taraki. He left the fourth member of his group, Wakil Hassan, to trip one or two of the motion detectors the SEALs had set up. This would create a small diversion before they fired on the COP. Just after midnight, Rabbani watched as Hassan purposely tripped one of the motion detectors and waited to see if there was a reaction. While he could see no movement from the base, he knew that he had their attention. He began to worry a bit if he was being too clever by trying to divert their attention.

He gave Hassan thirty minutes to work his way to a point near their position where they had agreed to meet after the attack. He then checked the distance and angle of his Zagan 82 mm mortar and dropped in the charge. As soon as the shell left the tube, the night sky lit up with .50 caliber tracer rounds coming from the COP and Rabbani and the two brothers dove for cover behind a group of large boulders. The first rounds of return fire scored a hit on the mortar tube, shredding it to pieces and throwing tiny bits of shrapnel throughout the area. The mortar round completely missed its mark on the COP, and bullets pounded off the boulders taking out chunks at a time as Rabbani and the Taraki brothers furiously crawled away from the killing zone.

Flairs shot into the air and lit up the landscape as the three Taliban fighters reached a narrow crevice against the hillside with enough cover to stand upright. As Nadir Taraki arose near the edge of the pass, a round bounced off the rocks taking a piece of flesh out of his shoulder and knocking off his wool pakol cap. He stifled a yelp and looked around frantically for his brother and Rabbani, spotting them squatted a few yards away. The three were still rattled by the speed and accuracy of the response from the COP when Hassan met them in the crevice.

"Well, I think that angered them as Mullah Karmal has wished," Rabbani blurted breathlessly. "They will be coming now. We must move quickly. Wakil, bury our two contact mines here to slow them down. Abdul, patch up your brother's shoulder so that he doesn't leave a blood trail. Allah be with us."

###

Back at COP Craver Marvel, the men and military working dog of First Squad, Second Platoon of SEAL Team 4 and their Afghani interpreter and guide were geared up and ready to go. Lieutenant Kelly took one last minute to do an equipment check and ensure that each team member had sufficient ammo and water. They would have to pursue the Taliban on foot since they would traverse rough terrain, cutting through some narrow hills and mountainsides where no vehicles could pursue. The team left the gate in a two-man, five-meter disbursement with Zip, Todd, and Fox on point.

God be with us, Kelly quietly prayed to himself as his team efficiently moved out of the COP heading towards the area of the mortar shot.

It took them ten minutes to get to where the shot had been launched.

"Damn! Those SAS boys plastered this place," Fox said as he reached what was left of the mortar tube and surrounding boulders.

Todd and Zip took little notice. Zip had his nose to the ground and tail in the air. He was memorizing the scents of the men who had only recently left the area.

"Zoek!" Todd told Zip.

Zip darted towards the spot where the three Taliban fighters had made their way to the narrow pass. The rest of the squad followed Todd's and Zip's lead. At the front of the pass, they found some blood splatter and a tattered gray pakol. Todd left it where it was while Zip buried his nose in it to fully burn the scent into his memory. There was a lot of loose stone and dirt along the path and Zip would easily be able to track the scent.

Lieutenant Kelly brought up the rear of the squad and approached Todd while Zip continued to gather all the smells of the site.

"Can he track them?"

Todd didn't reply to what he thought was an absolutely ridiculous question. He just pursed his lips in an obvious gesture of annoyance and shot Kelly a sideways glance.

"OK, OK, dumb question," Kelly conceded. "Get him moving."

"Revieren!" Todd commanded, giving Zip permission to pursue the enemy and to be prepared to attack.

Zip immediately went to work and plunged into the narrow passage of rock at a determined pace with the rest of the team right behind. He was almost in a full trot, fired up by getting the green light to actually use his prey drive. He was so focused on his task that his brain did not fully register the new smell that wafted in the night air. He loped directly alongside and beyond another smell—a smell he was trained to detect and give warning for. When he got three meters past the odor, his danger awareness kicked in and he suddenly spun around. Todd was about to take a step towards the danger. Zip froze and pointed back at Todd, but the message did not immediately resonate, as Todd proceeded forward.

Zip barked and, taking a full running start, launched himself through the air back to where Todd and the rest of the squad were patrolling. At top speed and with sure aim, Zip flew directly into Todd's chest with such a force that it knocked him backwards and into Fox and Boomer.

Todd caught Zip, and as he fell back into Fox, who fell into Boomer, who caught all three, he shouted, "Nobody move!" The ten of them froze in place.

Todd released his grip on Zip. The dog stood, planted his paws, and, with his whole body, rigidly pointed to an object within a meter of where Todd lay. Todd turned on his flashlight and could tell from the slightly mounded soil that it was a Russian-made PMN-2 antipersonnel mine with enough explosive charge to either kill or horribly wound at least two of them with one blast—especially in the narrow crevasse where they were sandwiched. Zip and Todd inched toward the mound and soon discovered the second mine. Then they slowly made their way to the end of the rock passage and looped back without finding any more surprises.

"That's it Lieutenant Kelly," Todd reported. "Just those two." His chin sank and he looked contrite. "That's on me Lieutenant. I got Zip moving too quickly and was so focused on catching those bastards that I neglected to have him sweep for booby traps first. I should have known better."

"It's my fault, too, Petty Officer. My attention was on the walls in this pass and not on what was on the ground in front of us."

"Awesome!" Boomer broke in sarcastically. "Now that we've established that we all suck, can we just hug it out and go get those sons of bitches? They owe me a new iPad!"

"Lieutenant Kelly," R.J. asked, "do you want to blow these things in place?"

"No. Just mark them. I think those guys are on the run now so let's not give any indication of position."

As the team gathered themselves and prepared to move again, Abby quietly pulled Penman aside. "Scott, have you ever seen a dog do that before? I mean he stopped and threw himself into his master to prevent him from stepping on that mine."

"I've never even *heard* of a dog doing something like that," Penman said. "It's not how they're trained. They're disciplined to identify and warn, not to intervene like that. Whatever Zip did, he did out of his pack drive and desire to protect the team."

"*Khodaye man* (My God)," was all that Abby could muster in reply.

The team got out of the pass in the hillside and Zip was now back on the scent and in pursuit of Rabbani and his three accomplices. Zip adeptly moved back and forth, availing a sense of smell 600 times more sensitive than a human. Nadir Taraki's distinctive scent was unmistakable and any attempts at feigning direction or other false movements were quickly discovered, and adjusted for. They were closing ground on Rabbani and his men, and Zip and the rest of the team could feel it.

###

It is physically harder to be the prey than to be the hunter, just as it is physically more demanding to play defense than offense in football. Rabbani, the Taraki brothers, and Hassan were feeling the pressure and quickly becoming exhausted. They had been told to make evasive maneuvers and lead the Americans on a goose chase, but their every trick was soon discovered and the distance between them and the Americans was diminishing. The noose was tightening. They were completely on the defensive and running for their lives. And yet they had to reach the safety of Bebiyal—on time—where Karmal and the rest of his forces would lie in wait to rescue them.

"We must get to Bebiyal and rest. The ruins will provide cover and there will be some supplies placed there in anticipation of our arrival," Rabbani told his men. "We will have to hold out until Brother Karmal arrives. We have weapons and ammunition and we will be strong." The words of encouragement from Tajwah Rabbani did not mask the tone of desperation in his voice.

###

"These guys are good, Lieutenant," Todd said matter-of-factly as the SEALs continued their pursuit. "But this is good ground to track on. Zip has their scent and they have a bleeder. It's only a matter of time. In fact I think we might only be a couple kilometers behind them."

"Agreed. They have to be going here." Kelly looked at his field map and pointed out the ruins of Bebiyal. We've funneled them into this area and that's the only close place that might give them any cover. Let's pick up the pace so they don't have too much time to think once they get there."

###

It was late morning by the time Rabbani reached Bebiyal and he and his colleagues were completely spent. They needed sleep and had not eaten in a full day. There was water and rations neatly concealed in the main structure of the ruins and overhead cover to protect them from the sun. Abdul Taraki checked his brother's wound and Hassan collapsed in the corner.

"Tajwah, how could they have followed us like that?" Hassan said as he wiped the sweat from his face. "They followed our every move and did not fall for any of our diversions."

"I do not know Wakil. We underestimated their ability to track us," Rabbani responded calmly. He surveyed the path they had just come down, looking for any sign of pursuant movement.

As he watched the horizon and thought of the progressions they had made, it came to him. *The dog.* Then he said out loud, "It is the dog. They have a dog that is able to follow us. I saw it in Darbat when they found our weapons. You three stink and the dog can smell you." He paused, eyes focused on the ridge above them. "I hope you had a good rest, because here they come."

Chapter 12
We Train for War and Fight to Win

A half mile away, Lieutenant Kelly looked down on the ruins through his binoculars and sighed. "Crap. We came up on this place too fast. They'll know we're here."

The SEALs were near the top of a gentle rise that sat between two virtually sheer walls of a valley. There was little vegetation on the hard shale rock that had crumbled and sloped from the valley walls. The ruins below that were once a village consisted of several shells of former buildings, with a large one in the center that was still mostly intact. It had a roof over it that was patched together from pieces of the other surrounding structures. This small complex sat in a flat area of the valley. About one hundred meters behind the main building was a dry creek bed that would fill up when the rains washed through the valley.

Strategically, Bebiyal was in a terrible spot. There were ledges and numerous points where they could get an easy advantage on the four Taliban insurgents dug into the main building. They could simply run a tactical belt around the structures and slowly squeeze until the men inside gave up or were killed. Unfortunately, Kelly didn't feel he had the time. As great an advantage as it was for his team, it was as bad as it could be if they were caught here. When he surveyed the area surrounding the ruins, he could see the way the valley made a cone his team could easily become trapped if they were caught in the wrong position. The place was like an eye of a needle and there was no way that air support could get to them if they needed help or a medical evacuation. Even though it was still early afternoon, the sun was already headed behind the valley walls and shadows fell across the landscape.

R.J. spoke up first as he surveyed the area. "Lieutenant, those guys picked a terrible place to stop. We can wait them out and pick them off individually."

"I don't know, Senior Chief," Kelly said. "If it's bad for them, it's bad for us. No, we need to be quick about it and get the hell out of here.

"Gentlemen, let's get this done. Angel, you and Doc are on the ridge to the right. Get yourselves into a position where you have eyes on that forward window. If anyone makes an aggressive move and sticks his head out, take it off. R.J. and Radar, flank the main building. Get to that other hut between the building and the creek bed. There may be a back way out that I can't see from here. Fox, Mitchell, Abby, and Zip will loop around to the small structure to the left of the big building. On my signal, Abby will call out to them giving them an opportunity to give themselves up. When they don't, we move in. Boomer, Penman, and I will flank the building from the right and cover the other structures. Angel and Doc, you have three minutes to get into position. We need to get a live one out of this if we can."

###

Tajwah Rabbani stared up at the position where the SEALs had been watching him. "Load up everything we have. Grab extra magazines. Now, Wakil and Abdul, you go to the cover on the left with the RPG. Nadir, you take the front window and I will cover the back. They will move for position and send some to flank us. Wakil and Abdul, I want you to wait for the first group to get in position in front of us and then deliver at least two rockets to their belly. After you have shaken them up, we will provide covering fire so that you can make it back here. We need to lower the numbers in our favor and give them some pause before they assault us, which they inevitably will do. We must buy some time. Now go, and Allah be with you."

###

Todd checked Zip's Kevlar flak jacket to make sure it was secure and Fox took the lead as they headed toward their specified position. The SEALs moved out and rolled quickly and stealthily into their positions, like small BBs in a child's game guided into their little cardboard cutout nesting spots, just as Kelly had mapped out.

As they crawled within thirty meters of the main structure, Fox noticed movement at their predetermined spot and whispered into his communications headset, "Um, Lieutenant, there seems to be no vacancy at our specified location. It looks like two guys with AKs and an RPG. We're kind of caught in the middle out here."

"OK. Stay put. We're almost in position. Angel, do you have eyes on?"

"Negative," the sniper replied. "The main building has me blocked."

Kelly quickly scanned for an alternative position for his small forward team. "To your right and twenty-five meters ahead is a bunch of blocks that looks like it was part of a wall. Can you make it there?"

"Not without being seen," Fox replied.

Todd and Zip were in a prone position about three meters left from where Fox was discussing options with Lieutenant Kelly. Abby was to Fox's right. "Stay still, Zip," Todd whispered in the dog's ear as Zip softly panted, waiting for his next command. "Jimmy, we can't stay here," he whispered to Fox, who only nodded in reply.

Lt. Kelly, Penman, and Boomer were settled into their position behind the main building where they were supposed to be and the others had successfully worked themselves into their strategic locations.

"Scotty, you're gonna have to do the talking. Tell them they are surrounded," Kelly said. Then he addressed Fox, Todd, and Abby. "When Penman starts talking, wait for an opportunity and then get to the wall."

"Copy that," the three murmured in unison.

Then Penman began to speak in his best Pashto, "Taliban insurgents, you are surrounded by ISAF Forces. Drop your weapons and come out."

Abdul Taraki and Hassan were caught off guard by the voice

coming from behind them and reflexively spun to see if they could find the source.

Fox saw their distraction, and it was the moment they needed.

"Go!"

The four were up and moving in a flash, heading to the wall in a full sprint, when Taraki and Hassan came to their senses and saw their movement. Abdul opened up with his AK 47, spraying bullets in the direction of the SEALs headed for cover.

"Wakil! Fire!" Rabbani screamed from the house.

Hassan leveled the RPG in the direction of the running figures and pulled the trigger. The high-pitched hiss and whistle of the igniting solid rocket fuel in the grenade filled the air, and the rocket took off from the launcher as the recoil kicked up a cloud of dust behind the two Taliban insurgents.

Todd, Zip, Abby, and Fox were in a mad dash for the blocks as the grenade came screaming in their direction.

"RPG!" Todd yelled and everyone dove to find what minimal cover was available. The rocket slammed into the ground fifteen feet from them sending rock and shrapnel flying. The shockwave of the blast knocked Zip sideways and he spun over on his back as pieces of hot metal imbedded into his flak jacket. Todd grabbed him by the corner of his jacket as he tumbled by and tucked the sixty-pound animal under his arm. The three men quickly rose to their feet and scrambled behind what was left of the wall.

AK 47 fire erupted from the building and the small outcrop, and pinged off the rocks around Todd's and Lieutenant Kelly's groups, effectively pinning them down for the time being.

R.J. and Radar returned fire from the left flank with R.J. focusing fire on the source of the RPG fire and Radar raking the main building.

Hassan loaded another rocket into the launcher and spun in the direction of the latest threat. He pulled the trigger and a second grenade burst from the launcher and slammed into R.J.'s and Radar's position. The two SEALs saw the incoming grenade and rolled behind and beneath the available cover as the ensuing explosion blew a hole out of the front wall of what was another small hut, causing it to collapse. What was left of the roof fell on top of them and they had to spend the next few seconds digging themselves out of the rubble.

Taking advantage of the confusion and cover from the smoke

and dust, Hassan and Abdul Taraki scrambled back to the main house and dove through the front entrance, desperate to find cover before the impending counter attack.

Behind the stone blocks that provided much-needed cover for Todd, Abby, Fox, and Zip, they tried to pull themselves together. Abby held his head to clear the ringing in his ears and deal with the pain of a ruptured eardrum while Fox dug a piece of shrapnel out of his leg. Todd tried to stop the gush of blood coming from just below his helmet line. A piece of flying rock had caught him on the left brow and he was wiping blood from his eye, trying to spot Zip and the others. Zip lay rattled, struggling to take deeper breaths. The impact of the shrapnel on his flak jacket and the force with which Todd grabbed up and carried him over the wall had bruised his ribs.

The gunfire from the house became more relentless as AK 47 fire riddled all three of the SEAL's locations surrounding the Taliban stronghold. R.J.' s and Kelly's positions were able to return fire but Todd, Abby, and Fox were pinned down.

Three hundred yards away from a concealed vantage point above the fray, Angel waited for his opening. The four Taliban were experienced fighters and knew how to remain properly concealed. Their earlier movements were effectively masked by the explosions, and the resulting debris kept Angel from getting off a proper shot. Now, they were viciously firing on his team and he needed one of them to make a mistake. He focused on the front window where Nadir Taraki was firing from, making things very difficult for Todd, Abby, and Fox.

Doc Burk was spotting, trying to find a good target. Angel patiently looked through the Leupold Mark 4 scope sitting atop of his Barret M82 A1 sniper rifle and quietly said, "Doc, they need to peek out of there to shoot but they have the windows blocked up with sandbags. I can't get a clear shot. How thick do you think those walls are?"

"I'd say about eight inches."

Angel made some fast calculations and assumptions in his head and peered through his scope, concentrating on the barrel of an AK 47 subtly protruding from the window. He could make out the angle of the barrel and estimated the distance to the butt of the rifle. He briefly took his eye out of the scope and then reacquired his target. Controlling his breathing, he slowly exhaled and squeezed the trigger. The .50 caliber projectile left the muzzle at 853 m/sec and slammed into the block frame of the window a third of a second later. The armor piercing round caused the mortar and stone to explode directly in front of Nadir Taraki's head—a large chunk of rock immediately fractured his skull. He collapsed to the floor and as blood filled his cranial cavity, the pressure increased on his brain and he began to convulse uncontrollably. In thirty seconds, he was dead.

"Target down," Angel reported calmly.

Chapter 13
The Success of Our Mission

Inside the shell-pocked house, Abdul Taraki screamed as he watched the life drain from his brother. Rabbani, who had heard the shot and subsequent scream, ran to the front of the building to see Nadir's body on the floor. There was no time for mourning and he said, "Abdul, your brother is a martyr and is now in paradise. If you don't wish to join him today, we must go."

Abdul Taraki said nothing but simply glared at Rabbani for a second and then followed him to the back of the house.

###

Kelly heard Angel's report and said to Fox and Todd over the comms set, "Did you guys hear that? Can you go?"

"Affirmative," Todd said as he secured his last piece of tape over the gauze to control his bleeding head.

Todd and Fox lobbed two grenades at the front of the house where Rabbani was and used the ensuing explosions to cover their movements. The four wounded SEALs took off for the entrance. When they reached the front, they stayed low and Fox immediately tossed in a flash bang. As soon as the charge detonated, Zip went through the door with Todd, Fox, and Abby right behind—their MP5-N submachine guns at the ready. As soon as he saw Nadir Taraki on the floor, Fox put two rounds into the body to ensure that he was no threat. They fanned out through the remaining rooms looking for the other three insurgents.

"Clear!" they repeated as they entered each of the rooms.

"Lieutenant," Todd began, "there's no one here. Just the Tali that Angel got."

Kelly didn't reply right away. He looked intently through his binoculars at the back of the house. Then he mentally traced a line from the rear wall. "Boomer!" he began to give orders. "You and Penman get to the creek bed now! They'll be coming your way. R.J., you and Radar cover the back of the house!"

Back inside, Zip was madly sniffing everything and moved to the back corner of the house. He noticed a prayer rug covering something and promptly signaled to Todd that he had found it. Todd pulled back the mat and a piece of board, exposing the entrance to a tunnel. "Abby, Fox," he said, "make sure this place is secure." Then he slung his machine gun, unholstered his Sig Sauer P226 handgun, whistled at Zip, and with the dog leading the way, they both vanished through the dark passage.

As soon as he dropped into the tunnel, Todd realized that he hadn't really thought this thing through. The diameter of the whole passage was only about a meter and he was crawling after the enemy in the dark. Zip was now ahead of him, hot on the scent of his prey, and there was no way he could keep up. It would be impossible to see a booby trap, and if the Taliban decided to leave a grenade behind they could bring the whole thing down on top of him. He wanted to call out to Zip and turn him around, but that would alert the insurgents that they had found the tunnel. This was the only chance that they still might surprise them.

Zip was operating on pure drive interaction. Just a few minutes ago he had been the hunted and now he was the hunter. He could easily move through the tunnel and was rapidly closing ground on his prey. His predator and fight drives were fully engaged, and he could smell the blood in front of him.

Ahead in the tunnel, Rabbani led the way with Abdul Taraki behind him and Hassan a fairly distant third, having been left to conceal the tunnel entrance before he moved. As Hassan crawled in terror, desperately trying to reach his colleagues, he heard something behind him. He sensed what was coming. Rabbani had told them about the dog and he had seen it running when he fired his RPG shot. It is said that the three things humans fear most are speaking in public, being trapped in a confined space, and being eaten alive by an animal. Hassan was experiencing the latter two and his hunger and exhaustion amplified his fear to a level of sheer panic. He tried to crawl faster as he heard the panting and the impact of Zip's paws striking the dirt and rock floor of the tunnel in a rhythmic beat. The echoes in the darkness terrified him as Zip's panting drew closer and closer.

In despair he called out, "Tajwah, please, help me!"

There was no answer; he was on his own. He tried to look behind him and, flipping over on his back, blindly fired his weapon into the darkness until he had emptied his magazine.

Twenty meters behind and closing the distance quickly Zip pushed forward, undeterred by bullets hitting the walls, floor, and ceiling of the tunnel. A shot whizzed dangerously close, clipping the tip of his ear, which only angered him. An aggressor was trying to injure him and his pack. Now all the elements of his training, prey, and fight drives were about to come to bear on the unfortunate flesh of Wakil Hassan. Before the echoes of the shots faded, Zip was on top of him, fangs bared. Hassan screamed in horror and could only throw his hands up in front of his face in defense. Zip latched on to the Taliban's forearm and, with 400 pounds of bite pressure, punctured his flesh and snapped his radius. Hassan's screams intensified as the animal incapacitated him and began clawing his way up his body to latch on to his throat.

Todd heard what was happening ahead of him and crawled as fast as he could. His eyes were adjusting and he could vaguely make out the silhouettes of the two figures. He could see that Zip was tearing into the human form beneath him. When he drew within six feet of the two he called Zip to halt the attack, and he immediately complied and moved back to Todd's position. Todd pinned Zip beneath him, targeted his sidearm at Hassan and fired two shots. The screaming ceased. Todd turned on his flashlight and made sure that the Taliban was dead. Then he and Zip backed their way out of the tunnel over the path they had come.

Near the end of the tunnel, Rabbani heard the screams and fatal shots, and immediately knew that Wakil Hassan had joined Nadir Taraki in death. He came to a solid wall and pushed hard. The wood covering began to move and as he shoved it out it fell away and the tunnel was flooded with daylight. He spilled out of the exit and tumbled into the bottom of a creek bed. As he tried to rise and adjust his eyes, he was pummeled by a charging body.

Boomer tackled the Taliban at full speed. The force of the unexpected impact knocked the wind out of Rabbani. He hit the ground with a force that separated his shoulder. Behind Rabbani, Abdul Taraki saw the ruckus by the opening and knew something was wrong. He made his way on his belly to the tunnel exit and saw Boomer over Rabbani, pinned on the ground. Taraki remained in a prone position and took aim with his weapon. He would never press the trigger. Twenty yards behind Boomer, Penman was also running down the bottom of the creek bed. He watched Boomer tackle Rabbani and saw the barrel of a rifle poking from a hole above. Penman delivered a burst of semi-automatic weapon fire into the hole and a torso slumped over, hanging out of the tunnel. The AK 47 slipped from Abdul Taraki's lifeless hands.

Kelly was not far behind and came up on them as Boomer yanked Rabbani to his feet. Rabbani winced in pain as Boomer dragged him by the collar to where Kelly and Penman were standing. Kelly demanded a status update from each group to ensure that the area was secure. Each team responded in the affirmative, as Zip and Todd emerged from the tunnel entrance back inside the house.

"Doc, get down here," Kelly ordered. "Angel, keep a lookout. Watch the north end of the valley. I have a feeling these guys were waiting for someone. R.J. and Radar, establish a perimeter. Stock and Penman, let's get this guy back up to the house."

Boomer hauled the Taliban insurgent out of the creek bed and back to the house in a most indelicate manner. Once they were all there, Kelly dismissed Boomer and sent him to join R.J. and Radar as sentries. Within a couple minutes, Doc arrived to evaluate the team's wounded. Todd said that he was fine and wanted him to look at Zip first but Doc would have none of it. He cleaned Todd's head wound, put him through a brief concussion evaluation, and pulled out a tube of super glue to seal the laceration. Then he turned his attention to Abby and Fox.

He patched up Fox's shrapnel wound and checked out Abby's ear. Once he was satisfied that, with the exception of Abby's ruptured eardrum, their injuries were relatively superficial, he bent down to look at Zip. The jagged flap that was once Zip's right ear looked worse than it really was, but infection was the real danger and Doc Burk cleaned the wound with some disinfectant. Then he made a rigid bandage around the damaged part of the ear using gauze and thin strips of wetted casting plaster. Doc Burk made sure to continue the examination of the dog by taking off his vest and feeling down the length of Zip's body to ensure there were no bullet holes or other puncture wounds.

"Check him close Doc." Todd said. He's tough and might not show any indications that he's injured."

"He's good Todd." Doc replied, "Just the messed up ear."

He then looked at Rabbani.

"His shoulder is separated. Boomer did quite a number on him," Doc said as he examined the Taliban.

"Pop it back in," Kelly said. "I need him mobile."

Doc did as instructed and, nodding at Fox, made Rabbani lie on a bench on his stomach. He knelt beside him while Fox held him down, then grabbed Rabbani's arm and swiftly, externally rotated the shoulder, pulling it down and away from the body. Rabbani screamed in pain as his upper arm bone moved back into his collarbone, then moaned in relief.

"Abby, find out who this guy is," Kelly snapped.

Abby posed the question in Pashto.

Rabbani only stared back with a scowl of pain and hatred on his face. He tilted his head to the side and his eyes opened slightly in recognition. "We know you. You are the Persian," Rabbani said. "The Master knows you too. He has special plans for you."

Abby scoffed and turned to Kelly. "We kept the right one alive, Lieutenant. He works for the man in the mountains and he's fairly high placed. He has access to information that others would not."

Rabbani understood English and was shocked that Abby was able to deduce so much from just a few sentences. A look of surprise came over his face and he was unable to wipe it off before he realized he had given himself away.

"And … he knows what we are saying," Abby added.

Rabbani kicked himself for being so clumsy but the pain, hunger, and exhaustion were taking a toll and he was becoming foolish.

"It does not matter," he spoke in English. "You will all be dead soon."

As if on cue, the voice of Angel Nakamura came over the comms set. "Lieutenant, I think this guy's dinner guests have arrived. Actually, it looks more like a banquet."

Chapter 14
We Demand Discipline. We Expect Innovation

Nur Mohammad Karmal looked down on the ruins of Bebiyal in disgust. His plans of ambushing the Americans had been ruined. He stood, his gaze transfixed on the main house and the group of SEALs guarding the outside, and his mind began turning. *How could they have caught Tajwah so quickly?* he wondered. *He is too good for that.* Then he glanced at the creek bed to see the limp body of Abdul Taraki still hanging from the tunnel entrance, and speculated if any of them were still alive.

In seconds, he snapped back to reality. "Abdur, ready the men," he ordered. "We must avenge our brothers."

###

Inside the house, Lieutenant Kelly was already at work.

"Angel, how far are they?"

"Still two kilometers."

"Where and how many?"

"From the north, like you thought. I can't tell how many but from some of the disbursement patterns of the ones I could see, I would say at least fifty and as many as a hundred."

"OK. We have a little time. Get the hell back here—everyone!"

The SEALs promptly assembled in the house with Angel joining about two minutes behind the others.

"Everyone, hydrate!" Kelly commanded. "The Tali, too. Then zip tie his wrists, gag him, and put a hood on him. He's coming with us. Abby, get him the hell out of here while we talk." Kelly pulled out his field map and continued as Abby shuttled Rabbani out of the house.

"We can't leave the way we came in. They have the angle on us and will cut us off before we get out of the valley. We have to cut back and through this pass—here." He pointed to a narrow gorge on the topographic field map. "If we can get through there before they get position, we can put some ground between them and us and get to here." He pointed to a space that was once the location of another combat outpost, abandoned for two years. "I don't know what we'll find there but the last drone reconnaissance I looked at showed that it still had some defensible coverage. Once we get there, R.J. should be clear of these damn mountains enough to establish communications and call for an evac.

"We're going to have to move fast. We need the remaining daylight and we can't let the Tali weigh us down. If Abby's right, he has too much information on that guy up there on the hill."

The team listened intently and while he talked they started their equipment checks. Todd was still bringing water for Zip, who greedily lapped at it. He knew Zip had to be exhausted, and was worried about heat stroke, knowing that dogs cannot dissipate heat from their bodies through sweat like humans do. Zip was built for acceleration and bursts of activities. He wasn't especially adept at marathons. Todd was a bit concerned that Zip might not make it to whatever was left of the COP that Kelly had lined up.

Kelly continued in full operational mode. "Everyone do a weapons and ammo check. Angel, get in a recon position and keep me up to date on their movements. Mitchell, you and Zip scrounge through this place and see what weapons are left. We could use an M60 or something close, and get Hancock that RPG with about five grenades."

Zip and Todd went to work and quickly found a cache of weapons. Among them was an old but well-maintained Russian PKM machine gun with about a thousand rounds of ammunition. They also found the additional grenades for the RPG launcher and got them back to the rest of the team.

"Alright, good work," Kelly said. "Now let's get the hell out of here. Mitchell—you, Robbins, and Zip are on the point. Blaze us a trail to that COP. Don't worry if you put distance between us and yourselves. We need you to get to a position where R.J. can get in touch with Bagram and get us some support. Penman—I want you and Abby in the middle with the Tali. Keep him moving and keep him quiet. We can only move as fast as you can make him go. Doc—you and Stock are on a ten-meter spread on the right flank. Hancock and Fox—you're on the left. I'll bring up the rear with Angel. We'll do what we can to slow them down and make them think about their moves. Is that all clear?"

"Aye Aye," was the uniform response from the team.

They moved out in the formation that Kelly had lain out. He and Angel lagged behind to rig enough thermite charges to ensure that the remaining weapons in the house would never be used again. As Todd, R.J., and Zip moved forward, they heard the controlled explosion signaling the destruction of the weapons and probably the remaining structure. They didn't bother to look behind.

"R.J., how far to the COP?"

"Just over six kilometers. "But it's over some pretty effed-up terrain. I'm a little worried about getting to a position where we can get a satellite connection. Even then, we'll be on our own for nearly forty minutes before they get to us. A lot can happen in a firefight that long. How's Zip doing?"

"Better than I expected. He's keeping up and he's actually still alert. This is one tough dog."

"Well, you trained him. He's one of us." They continued their hike. "Hey Mitchell, did you ever notice that there's nobody from Texas in the unit?"

Todd was caught a little off guard by the sudden change of subject. "What?"

"We got nobody from Texas. I mean, look at it. Every military unit has *somebody* from Texas. Marcus Luttrell—Texas. Chris Kyle—Texas. Audie Murphy—Texas. Hell, it seems like every war movie ever made has some dude named Tex in it. Not us. We're spread from all around the country but not one guy from the biggest state in the lower forty-eight. Isn't that something?"

Todd thought about it for a second and then replied, "That's not really true, R.J. Zip is from Texas."

"What? No he's not. He's Belgian or German or something like that."

"Nope. He's part Belgian Malinois and part German Shepherd but he was actually born and bred at a kennel in Texas. That means he's a Texan. So we do have a Texan in the unit."

"Well, I stand corrected," R.J. conceded. "He should have that little lone star flag patch on his vest."

The three SEALs pressed forward putting ground between them and the rest of the team. They were about thirty minutes into the march when they began to hear sporadic gun fire and explosions behind them. It was the distinctive sound of the blending of U.S. and Russian weapons, and they couldn't tell which was more dominant.

"Sounds like Kelly and Angel are giving them something to think about," Todd said.

"I wonder if the rest are moving forward," R.J. replied. "Let's keep going and get there so we can cover them as they come in."

They proceeded through the gorge and up and down the rough terrain for the next two hours before they came to a clearing, and within eyesight of Combat Outpost Walker. There were still some concrete barricades and fortified observation turrets intact. There was good frontal protection with a clear killing ground of about three hundred meters. However, the back of the COP was completely exposed. The walls had been dismantled and any salvageable metal and other scrap had been removed. And there was something else.

"Dammit," R.J. said as he scanned the base through his binoculars. "There's some goddamned goat herders there, just hanging out."

Both R.J. and Todd knew that it was impossible to tell whether they were friendly or hostile. They couldn't move towards the base either aggressively or passively, knowing that the wrong choice could be disastrous.

"See if you have enough clearance to reach Bagram," Todd suggested.

R.J. turned on the Inmarsat radio, which still had good battery power, and smiled as he got a signal. "Sierra Tango Two to Bravo Alpha One. Sierra Tango Two to Bravo Alpha One." He paused and waited for the reply. After seconds that seemed like hours, it came crackling back.

"This is Bravo Alpha One. Go Sierra Tango Two."

Robbins continued, "Troops in Contact. I repeat. Troops in Contact. Coordinates 34°55'08"N by 70°55'56"E. Say again 34°55'08"N by 70°55'56"E. About a hundred hostiles in pursuit."

###

Commander Heard had already arrived in the situation room at Bagram and was studying a satellite photo of the coordinates and adjacent topographic map of the area. He recognized what he was looking at.

"That's COP Walker. It's got enough flat area to land the helos and provide an evac. Get the pararescue team ready to go in five mikes and alert an Apache for support. Move!" Heard got on the radio. "Sierra Tango Two, this is Bravo Alpha One. Understood. Help is on the way. Sit tight."

"Understood," the voice of Senior Chief Petty Officer Robbins crackled back. There was nothing more that needed to be said. Kelly's men would have work to do in anticipation of the rescue.

###

While R.J. was radioing in his report, Todd was hatching a plan to get the herders out of the way without being aggressive.

"R.J., get down outside the front wall and try not to let them spot you. When I radio, set off a smoke grenade and draw their attention. Zip and I will loop up by the goats and scramble them. When the herders go after them, you get inside the COP and cover us while we get back. Then we'll have a defensive position where we can keep them off if need be until the rest of the boys arrive."

"Makes sense. Let's get moving. The others should be coming up behind us any time now."

R.J. moved out and stealthily made his way around to the front of the COP. Todd and Zip moved up along the slope of the hill to a point where they could slip down to the edge of the herd. The herders were mostly on the far side of the goats, resting and not paying much attention to what was going on. They had heard the gunfire in the distance and were discussing what might be happening, apparently without much concern.

"OK, R.J. Fire it up."

R.J. pulled the pin on the grenade and threw it about twenty yards to his right. The green smoke billowing out of the grenade instantly caught the attention of the herders. Todd told Zip to stay and left him right on the lower edge of the herd as he made his way to the upper edge. When he got to his spot, he called out to Zip with the command to come. Zip sprang into action and the sudden presence of a dog caused the entire herd to take off, funneling through a hole between Todd and Zip. As Zip continued to run and cut across the edge of the goats towards Todd, the bleating herd ran. Zip changed direction a few times to keep them moving away from the COP. The herders, whose attention now shifted toward the pandemonium, ran after the animals to try and get them under control. As soon as they did, R.J. was up and moving. He scaled the front wall of the COP and plopped down inside. When Todd saw he was in, he whistled for Zip and they both took off back toward the COP. They all made it inside before the herders could figure out what had happened. They then took up positions and gave indications that the herders were not to attempt to come back.

As the annoyed herders moved the goats farther away and back up into the hills, R.J. saw Abby and Penman emerge from the pass with Rabbani in tow. Right behind them were Radar and Fox. Just as they got to the wall of the COP, Boomer and Doc Burk came out of the pass at a full sprint. Boomer barreled into the base just ahead of Doc.

"Get ready," he gasped, trying to catch his breath. "They're right on our ass! Angel and the Lieutenant are coming."

R.J. stepped up and took command. "Listen! Radar, you get that RPG trained on the pass and as soon as they're clear, fire one straight into it. Fox, get the PKM set up on that right turret. Cut down anything that comes out of that pass after the L.T. and Angel. They'll think twice before they send anyone else through. It might take them a little time to find a work-around and give us what we need to get a defense set up. Hell, the cavalry might even arrive by then."

"Abby, you get our guest down and out of the way where he can't cause any trouble. Mitchell," R.J. spoke loudly and clearly enough for Rabbani to hear, "get Zip on him to make sure he stays put. If he moves, have him tear his throat out."

The team did as ordered and was set up and waiting for Kelly and Angel to clear the pass. For five long minutes there was silence. No gunfire or explosions or any indication of movement from either the Taliban or the two remaining SEALs of the squad. Suddenly, Kelly and Angel came flying out of the pass, running for their lives. They had stripped off their packs and nearly all their equipment and were dressed only in their BDUs. When they were only about twenty yards away from the pass, Radar could see a group of Taliban also emerge. He took aim and delivered an RPG grenade directly into the narrow entry of the pass. The ensuing explosion shook the ground all the way back to the COP and the concussion loosened massive pieces of rock which rained down on the Taliban caught in the pass. The cries of the wounded buried beneath the rubble let the team know they had effectively eliminated the immediate threat to Kelly and Angel.

"Nice shot Radar!" Boomer exclaimed as Fox opened fire on the pass, making sure that no one else came out.

Fox efficiently covered the Lieutenant and Chief Petty Officer as they scrambled into the COP. Kelly had not even caught his breath before he began spitting out orders and demands for status updates. "Is anyone injured?"

"Just banged up. We're good," Doc said.

"OK. How are we fixed for defense?"

"Well Lieutenant," R.J. said, "it could be worse. The frontal approach is solid with a good killing zone. Also, the LZ is in good shape. The goat herders kept it flat and bare. But our ass is exposed at the flank. Most of the barrier has been stripped. Help is on the way and I anticipate arrival in twenty-five minutes."

"What's our weapon and ammo status?"

R.J. continued, "A bit light but we didn't have to use any on our trip here so we have a good small arms compliment. We sure could use some firepower, though. Our effective range is limited with the MP5s. We have whatever's left of the rounds in the PKM and four more grenades for the RPG. How about you guys?"

"Well, we had to drop nearly everything and use most of our ammo," Kelly said. "We rigged a few surprises for those guys and we think we got a few of them on the way here. At least we slowed them down and made them think a little bit. Angel has about thirty rounds left for the .50 cal. I'm down to one magazine and a couple of clips for my sidearm."

Having assessed the current situation, Kelly set about making plans for the arrival of the evac helicopters. "They know we're watching the pass entrance now and we've got that covered. They're moving for position and will be popping out along that ridge up there." He pointed and pulled out the field map once again to begin studying. "As fast as they move, they'll get to a position near our flank in less than ten minutes if they continue along this path—here. They're going to start a frontal assault soon while they make the flanking maneuver. They'll try to keep us busy and distracted until they get here—," he said, pointing to an area on the map directly behind the landing zone.

"Angel was right. We think there are nearly one hundred of them and we won't be able to stop them from getting around to our flank. There's just too much usable cover. Our focus has to be on keeping the LZ clear when the helos get here. I want to create a number of fallback positions through the COP. When the helos are within two kilometers, we'll abandon the COP and create a perimeter defense from the gullies on the edge of the LZ. As soon as the choppers touch down, they're going to draw all the fire so we have to move fast. Hopefully, they have an Apache or two providing cover, so that should help."

Kelly had barely finished when an RPG round slammed into the frontal barricade, just as predicted. Then the small arms fire began to intensify and draw the team's attention to the forward position. Kelly used Fox and Angel to keep them at bay with machine gun and sniper rifle fire while Boomer and Doc covered the left side. Hancock and Penman on the right were fending off probing attacks from the groups of Taliban insurgents. They were systematically advancing and retreating; gauging the stability of defenses and tempting the SEALs to use up their ammunition. It was an effective strategy. While this was going on, Kelly and Abby were evaluating the LZ at their flank to make sure they had enough room for the helos and adequate cover for the evacuation.

Todd knelt by Rabbani, who lay prone in what was left of a corner wall, and readied his weapon. "Not a word, my friend, not a word," he said.

The Taliban trembled involuntarily. Any pain he might have had in his shoulder was overridden by dread, as he felt Zip's hot breath on the back of his neck and listened to the panting sound coming from much too close to his ear.

After about ten minutes into the firefight, the attack suddenly stopped. There was no further movement from the area around the COP.

"Weapons status!" Kelly barked, taking advantage of the lull in fighting. The reports came back over his comms set that the team was holding its own, but had only enough ammo to resist just one or two more assaults, depending on the numbers sent at them. Kelly realized how desperate the situation had become.

Abby, do you play chess?" Kelly asked.

"Sir?" Abby was taken aback at why Kelly would be discussing games at a time like this.

"Chess—Do you play chess?"

"Why yes. However, I haven't been able to find the time lately."

"They've got the pieces and position. We'll need to buy some time and allow the choppers to get here. I figure we can make about five more counter moves before checkmate."

Chapter 15
I Am Never Out of the Fight

The eerie lack of movement made the team nervous, and the sound of the wind and the dust kicking up made the COP look like something out of a Sergio Leone western. Then Kelly heard the clank of bells and the bleating of goats, and he caught sight of the herd that Zip and Todd had chased away.

"What the hell?" he mumbled to himself before snapping, "Mitchell! Get up here!"

Zip had sensed the presence of the herd, too. He rose from his crouch over Rabbani and turned his attention to the goats ambling back towards the open area in the perimeter of the COP. The fur on his black zigzag stood on end and his ears perked. His eyes, squinting slightly and intent on the moving animal mass flowing back in his team's direction, darted. He began to growl.

"Boomer, keep an eye on this jagoff for me," Todd shouted. "Let's go, Zip."

When they arrived, Kelly quizzed Todd. "What do you make of this?"

"That's the herd that R.J., Zip, and I chased away before the rest of you got here. Something's wrong. Zip is on edge."

"I see that. This is damned peculiar. I know the Taliban is using them to mask movement, but we can't waste more ammo just to make mutton. Let's send Zip in there to scatter them and see what they're hiding.

"Hancock and Stock get back here! It's going to get busy in a minute. Abby, go back there with the Tali and keep him quiet."

Todd gave the order to Zip to pursue, and he took off over the forty meters into the heart of the goats, separating them straight down the middle. As the frightened animals fled from the dog, Taliban fighters hiding in the herd were taken off guard and exposed to the waiting SEALs with weapons trained right on them. Before the SEALs could fire off a shot, Zip tore into the first Taliban he reached, knocking him to the ground and clamping down on his arm while violently snapping his head from side to side. The sudden appearance of the dog startled the other insurgents in the group. As the goats scrambled to escape the snarling animal, the Taliban found themselves completely exposed.

"Take 'em!" Kelly ordered, and the SEALs opened up on the Taliban with precise fire, cutting ten of them down before they knew what was happening.

Zip had his prey pinned and subdued as Todd rushed from the back of the COP and towards the spot where Zip was flopping up dust with the insurgent, shouting "Zip! Release!" Zip immediately let go and charged back to Todd's side. As the insurgent attempted to rise, Todd put two shots into his chest.

Chaos broke out at COP Walker. The Taliban insurgents began advancing from all sides and the remaining fifteen left alive in the goat herd charged towards the open back of the COP and the SEALs. It was a bizarre mixture of explosions, smoke, weapons fire, and the integration of panicked livestock with Taliban insurgents and Navy SEALs engaged in close quarter combat. Kelly shouted, "Fallback position one!" and the SEALs moved to the cover of the predetermined location inside the COP perimeter. Fox and Angel kept their attention forward as the Taliban breached the walls, methodically picking them off as they attempted to enter the COP. Immediately behind them, the rest of the group was dealing with a more immediate threat. The Taliban survivors of the goats herd trick were now within the perimeter with the rest of the SEAL Team. Kelly was down to his last clip and the rest of the group was assailing the attackers within a few feet of them.

Todd and Zip hit one of the Taliban head on. Todd threw a shoulder block into him knocking him off his feet while Zip pinned him to the ground. Todd drew his field knife and thrust it under the insurgent's ribcage, through his liver and puncturing his left lung. He held him down for several seconds and felt his chest collapse as the air drained from the body.

R.J. heard the sound of the approaching choppers and established contact. "Echo Tango One this is Sierra Tango Two. What is your status?"

"Sierra Tango Two this is Echo Tango One. We are two klicks out and have you in sight."

"Be advised Echo Tango One, the LZ is hot and our position is being overrun. Have the Apache concentrate fire within the COP on the approach. We will be under cover. Anyone in the open is to be considered hostile."

"Roger that Sierra Tango Two. Thirty seconds out, get your boys down."

"Lieutenant!" R.J. shouted into his comms set. "Thirty seconds!"

Kelly commanded, "Everyone to the LZ and stay low! They're going to light this place up! Move!"

The team began scrambling for the LZ, fighting their way through the few remaining Taliban attacking their flank. Abby and Penman dragged Rabbani, now suffering the effects of shock, towards the LZ. As Radar covered them, an AK 47 round struck him below his body armor, shattering his hip, and he crumbled to the ground. Doc Burk and Fox spun around and grabbed Radar, pulling him into the gulley beside the LZ. Just as they tumbled over the edge, another round let loose, hitting Fox in his Kevlar vest. It didn't fully penetrate the vest, but the impact sent him flying backwards into the gulley and he struck his head against a rock at the bottom. Right behind them zoomed Penman. Abby brought up the rear, yanking Rabbani and throwing him down into the pit with the others.

On the other side of the LZ, Kelly, R.J., Angel and Boomer dove for cover, with Todd and Zip tumbling in after them. Just as Todd hit the dirt, an Apache helicopter opened up on the COP with a rain of bullets from its 30 mm M230 chain gun, peppering the entire area at a rate of 625 rounds per minute and creating a massive cloud of dust. Taliban bodies fell like marionettes being cut from their strings. Behind the Apache were two UH 60 Blackhawk helicopters carrying an Air Force Pararescue "PJ" squad to assist with the evacuation. After the Apache potently secured the COP, the first Blackhawk touched down near Doc Burk's position. The PJs jumped out of the chopper and bolted towards Doc to assist with moving the two wounded SEALs and the Taliban captive to the waiting chopper. The second helicopter, coming in about a quarter mile behind the first, appeared to be landing considerably behind the first—leaving about forty yards between it and Kelly's position.

Kelly saw the Blackhawk descending and was dismayed at the distance between them. "Dammit! Everybody go!"

Todd and Zip were the first ones out of the gulley. "Zip go!" Todd screamed.

Zip galloped off towards the chopper, putting distance between himself, Todd and the rest of the team. As he neared the dirt where the helicopter was about to land, a Taliban fighter rose from his concealment within the ridgeline and fired an RPG round at the second Blackhawk. Zip heard Kelly screaming for everyone to hit the ground. The trail of smoke made by the burning propellant traced across the landing zone straight to the back end of the vulnerable helicopter in front of him. The flaming ordnance smashed into the tail rotor and exploded, heaving the chopper forward towards Zip and the rest of his SEAL team. Zip barked frantically at the out-of-control chopper, as it spun and lurched toward the ground.

Despite the pilot's fierce attempt to regain control, the composite material rotors ploughed into to the dirt, and the doomed helicopter crumbled like a child's toy, its splintering rotor blades flying about the LZ as the crew ejected from the open side door. The chopper nose pitched into the ground, crushing the cockpit and breaking the pilot's back, as the full force of the collapsing nose slammed into the copilot's chest and killed him instantly.

What was left of the tail boom violently swung around towards Zip, striking him on the hind quarters and throwing him fifteen feet through the air into a shallow ditch at the side of the landing zone.

"Zip!" Todd screamed as he pulled himself from the ground and ran towards the crash site. He hadn't traveled more than a couple of steps when another RPG round came screaming in, and slammed directly in front of him throwing him backwards. Shrapnel tore into his flesh and flak jacket, and the explosive shockwave ripped the helmet from his head.

The pararescue team from the first helicopter scrambled to respond to the crash site with Doc Burk and Penman. They grabbed the injured chopper pilot as the PJ team from the downed helicopter tried to reorient themselves and get back into action. While the PJs pulled the copilot's body from the wreckage, Boomer and Angel latched onto Todd and unceremoniously dragged him along the ground, determined to make their way back to the first chopper despite increasing small arms fire that riddled the landing zone. The Apache support helicopter spun towards the source of the RPG rounds and fired two Longbow Hellfire missiles into the position as it began taking hits from escalating automatic weapons fire.

"Let's go! We need to get the hell out of here!" Chief Warrant Officer Mark Sherman screamed as the SEALs charged his chopper, climbing in through the side door. As they piled in, Boomer and Angel rolled a disoriented Petty Officer Mitchell into the increasingly crowded space. Kelly was the last to board, pausing with one foot on the skid and staring back at the crash site despite Sherman's urging to move it. Kelly remained fixated on the crash debris, looking for any sign of movement. There was nothing. Then he reluctantly climbed on with the rest of his team, still scanning the site for any glimpse of his missing team member.

The helicopter was loaded beyond its safe weight limit and was struggling to get off the ground. The side door gunner and the Apache were suppressing some of the incoming fire, but bullets were still bouncing off the chopper as it struggled to gain altitude. One of the PJs let fly a string of profanities and grabbed his knee as they spun away from the source of the hostile fire and finally climbed towards safety at an agonizingly slow rate.

As the Blackhawk moved out of the valley, Todd started to come to his senses. "Where's … Zip?" His thick words hung in the air. He heard no response—just the rhythmic sound of helicopter rotor blades. He struggled to focus, and as his vision improved he saw the faces of his team and friends as they glanced at him, and then quickly averted their eyes.

###

At what remained of COP Walker, the K9 U.S. Navy SEAL known as Zip lay wounded among the burning wreckage, shell casings, and bodies of his enemies. The scent of his team and the sound of helicopters faded into the chilling air and darkening sky of the Korengal Valley as he realized they had left him behind. He was alone and, for the first time since Manny Blanco threw him out of the helicopter, he was afraid.

Chapter 16
In the Worst of Conditions

As the Blackhawk drew close to Bagram Air Base, Todd became more lucid. When he realized that Zip was not with them, he begged Lieutenant Kelly to turn the chopper around. Oblivious to the situation around him, he became more and more inconsolable as Kelly continued to ignore him. Finally, his frustration boiled over and he became confrontational, cursing at Kelly and hurling insults at him; questioning his courage for having left without Zip.

Boomer shot Todd several warning looks as his brazenness elevated precariously close to the degree where it could be inferred as an attempt to incite mutiny. Finally, Boomer decided that he had to step in, physically. He rolled on to Todd, pinning him to the floor of the chopper. Todd groaned, but went silent as the force of Boomer's huge frame drove pieces of shrapnel further into his legs and arms. His head throbbed with pain.

"Todd," Boomer spoke in a clear, firm voice, his lips close to Todd's ear. "Look around this chopper. There's blood everywhere. One of the pilots is dead and another one can't feel his legs. Mikey Hancock is hurt real bad and Doc is trying to keep him alive. Fox is busted up, too. One of the PJ's kneecaps is plastered to the ceiling.

This machine is overloaded and the Chief Warrant Officer flying it is doing everything he can just to keep us in the air. And on top of all that, we have a Tali on board who has valuable information." Then he added as he exerted all of his weight on top of Todd for emphasis, "Now—stop being an idiot!"

Todd started to come to his senses and take in the gravity of the situation. "OK," he wheezed. Boomer rolled off of him and Todd looked about the helicopter, taking in the grim scene and the looks on the men's faces. Finally, he caught sight of Kelly, who was glaring at him with fury in his eyes. Todd looked back, completely disheartened and cowed by the rebuke.

Kelly's rage gradually tempered to empathy. He sat back and closed his eyes as the weight of the decision to leave one of his team behind began to fall over him.

###

In the rubble of COP Walker, Abdur Rahman was poking through the wreckage of the downed Blackhawk looking for anything salvageable when, out of the corner of his eye, he caught movement in a shallow ditch. He looked in and saw what appeared to be an animal carcass, half buried under pieces of helicopter debris, rock, and dirt. At first, he thought it was one of the goats caught in the crossfire of the battle. But then he noticed the shape of the head and the bandaged ear tip, and he realized it was the mongrel that the Americans had with them. He had glimpsed it during the fight and even watched it attack one of his countrymen. A cruel, crooked smile passed across his lips as he pulled out his pistol and took aim at the animal's head.

"Abdur! What are you doing?" The quiet but forcefully distinctive voice of Nur Mohammad Karmal interrupted his actions.

Rahman, startled by the sound of Karmal's voice, could not believe that he had come up on him so stealthily and was standing directly behind him. "It is the dog of the Americans," he replied. "I saw this beast attack our men and I am about to extract vengeance in the names of our fallen brothers. Then I am going to cut off his ears and send them back to their base."

"Vengeance can take many forms, my friend," Karmal said. "Dig him out and determine the extent of his wounds. He may be of use to us."

Rahman was bewildered by Karmal's comment, but knew better

than to question God's Warrior, and so promptly obliged the order.

###

When the helicopter landed at Bagram, the wounded were quickly transferred to the infirmary. The severely wounded, including Radar, would be relocated to Germany for more extensive medical treatment. Fox, Todd, and the rest of the team could be treated on the base.

Even after they landed, Todd implored Lieutenant Kelly to assemble a rescue team and return for Zip. Eventually, the doctors sedated him so they could treat his head wound and remove the pieces of shrapnel that riddled his body. He would sleep for a full twenty-four hours. When he awoke, Todd was fighting concussion symptoms. He found that counting the numerous stitches in his body from where the RPG fragments were dug from his flesh helped him concentrate but he was still in considerable agony. "Excuse me." Todd shouted, "Can someone get me some aspirin or something? I'm in alotta pain here."

"Well you got alotta holes in ya." The attending nurse responded while mimicking him.

"You're a lucky man," she continued. "We pulled a fragment out of your flak jacket that was as big as an iPhone—would have gone straight into your heart. You just lay there and relax. These are mostly superficial, we'll have you back out there again in no time. Just as soon as you can pass the concussion protocol."

"How long will that take?"

"Depends on you and how much that brain of yours sloshed around in your skull—Maybe a week, maybe two."

During that time, the mission debriefing and interrogation of Tajwah Rabbani was in full swing. Lt. Kelly reviewed all of the particulars with Commander Heard—and the CIA special agent assigned to the Kunar province. Kelly was not particularly thrilled to be back in her presence. But Jennifer Kennedy was a particularly good interrogator and he had no say in the matter.

The CIA sent Agent Kennedy to Kunar for a number of reasons. She had been identified by the agency shortly after high school for her adeptness at communication and psychology. An unusually quick study, she earned undergraduate degrees in the unique combination of psychology and linguistics and a master's degree in international relations within four years. During her time in school, she also quietly trained with the CIA, focusing on

Afghanistan and Pakistan.

Her especially high IQ and academic prowess came at the expense of emotion and compassion. Her supporters, however, viewed this as an asset since she appeared to be unflappable. She was patient, persistent, could break down most barriers during the course of an interrogation, and was particularly adept at culling intelligence and making solid assessments. Her critics saw her as just another CIA robot with no amity for the people of the region or the lives affected by her work.

Rabbani was going to be a tough nut to crack but Kennedy was pertinacious. Within minutes of the Blackhawk landing earlier in the week, she had demanded that he be whisked away to an isolated portion of the base with the highest level of security. Rabbani was kept in a windowless cell, and in a constant state of disorientation. When he was permitted to sleep, it was during strange times so as to completely confuse his circadian rhythm and prevent him from entering a deeper, restful, REM sleep. The temperature of the room was constantly adjusted to be either too hot or too cold. Different, irritating noises were pumped into the space at all hours—the sounds of an infant crying, city traffic, or vuvuzelas (those tacky plastic horns blown during South African soccer games). Kennedy allowed Rabbani to stew in this environment while she did her research.

She pored over the notes on the mission and attacks at COP Craver Marvel and COP Walker. She interviewed Lieutenant Kelly, Abdul Ashkilani, and Scott Penman extensively about the events that had transpired, as well as information collected during their visits to the various villages in the valley. Later, she assessed other intelligence resources; those that no one but she and a select few others in the world could access. In the end, she narrowed down the actual identity of her captive to one of three choices. She had to make an educated guess as to which individual was correct before she started the interactive portion of the interrogation. If she was wrong in her guess, she would give Rabbani the advantage since he would know that she did not know who he was and, more importantly, who he was associated with. However, if she was right, she would have the upper hand and Rabbani would instantly be put on the defensive and therefore more apt to make a mistake. In the end, she felt confident that she had enough to give it a shot.

Agent Kennedy asked Abby to join her for the interrogations.

She felt that if she had someone in the cell with her who was intimate with the region and recent events, she could more quickly gauge lies from the truth. Abby was happy to oblige. Two hours before the interview began, she adjusted the temperature in Rabbani's cell to a consistent seventy degrees. She also directed that all artificial noises be turned off so that there would be complete silence with the exception of the buzzing of one fluorescent light positioned directly above his head. She ordered the cell emptied—the only furniture to be left in the room was a stool. Rabbani was told to sit there and not move.

When Kennedy entered the room some time later, she motioned for a chair and table to be brought in for herself, set up between her and Rabbani. She was dressed plainly in gray cargo pants and gray button down shirt with no labels or other identifying marks. A security guard followed her, and Abby followed the guard. The table was considerably higher than the legs of the stool where Rabbani was seated, forcing him to look over the table and up at Kennedy. It would be especially insulting for a Muslim male to be put in such a subservient position.

Abby stayed in the shadows, but not to hide himself. He was instructed to never really come forward in order to keep Rabbani guessing as to whether or not it was actually he who interrogated him first at Bebiyal. Abby was to listen and take mental notes and give Kennedy information as to when Rabbani was lying—if he eventually did decide to speak.

She took her time before sitting by circling him a number of times, taking notice of his posture and facial expressions. The more mental stress she could place on him, the better she would be able to control the situation. Finally, she pulled out the chair and sat down across from him.

"Tajwah Rabbani," she began in English. "Your life as you have known it is over. There is no hope for you. No one knows where you are and no one is coming for you—ever. We will not exchange you for anyone—you have no value. When we are done with you here, you will be moved to a detention facility in another land where you will never have contact with any of your family or countrymen again. You will spend the rest of your life not knowing where you are and with very little human contact. Let's just get that out of the way right now. However, there is hope for your family."

The exhausted Rabbani looked up at her, somewhat surprised

that they had discovered anything about him without ever asking him a question.

"So, this is what we have for you," she continued. "If you cooperate, we will ensure that your family in Khost is told that you are safe and we will arrange for their care. We will do this skillfully so that there will be no suspicion that you have given us information. If you do not cooperate, we will allow it to leak that you have capitulated and that you are a traitor to your Taliban brothers. We will also leave a very clear trail to your family with indications that they abetted you in an effort to gain your release. This will be done in a subtle but cogent manner." Kennedy purposely used the bigger words to confuse Rabbani and keep him guessing.

Without another word, she stood, motioned to the guard to remove the table, chair, and stool, and walked out the cell door allowing it to slam especially hard behind her.

Tajwah Rabbani was left alone on the bare floor of the cell. He was a conglomeration of negative emotion. Fear, anger, despair, hatred, loneliness, and dejection were all magnified by his environment, pain and complete physical depletion. He wept, curled in a fetal position, as the temperature once again began to drop and the sound of vuvuzelas filled the space.

In a room adjacent to the holding cell, Jennifer Kennedy dispassionately watched the display on CCTV with Abby. Then, without making eye contact she said, "We will do this for three more days. Then you will talk to him."

###

In the remote mountains of the Korengal Valley, rain began to fall. The steady downpour on his exposed body pulled Zip back to consciousness. With each moment, he became more cognizant of his condition. He had never been so thirsty but he could not drink any of the water falling around him because his muzzle was taped closed. Only the tip of his tongue stuck out between his incisors and canine teeth, and he found it difficult to turn his head to allow the drops to hit it. He was pinned nearly to the ground by a heavy metal collar and chain and could lift his head only with great effort. The chain was connected to a steel rod driven into the hard, packed soil. The rest of his body was in agony. His ear was bleeding, his ribs still hurt and, as he tried to stand, an excruciating pain shot through his hip. It intensified as he turned himself to see that half of the fur on his tail had been burned off, and he could smell his own scorched flesh. He stood only for a moment before shuddering and collapsing back to the ground. The mud formed around his beaten body and the rain intensified.

###

Todd sat quietly on a picnic table under a shelter outside the barracks at Bagram, watching the rain; apathetically staring at the drops bouncing off the edge of the airfield tarmac. When he cleared his concussion evaluation and was allowed to return to the squad, he received the news that a Marine Recon platoon went back to COP Walker the day after the attack. They searched the area and helicopter wreckage but could find no sign of a dog. They couldn't really be sure of anything because there were burnt carcasses of animals that had been caught in the firefight scattered in with the mess of the battle remnants. Some were mutilated so badly that they couldn't really be sure of the species. The general conclusion was that Zip had been killed in the crash of the Blackhawk and incinerated to a degree that could not allow him to be identified or retrieved.

The team had given Todd his space, but they felt it was time to bring him back into the fold. Naturally, the task would fall to Boomer. Without acknowledging his arrival, Todd continued to stare out at the rain and began to speak before his friend even sat down on the bench next to him.

"They didn't look hard enough Boomer. They should have found something. His jacket or tags—something! We have to go back and make sure."

"Hey brother," Ted said sympathetically, "You and I both know that's just not possible. Everyone here is on alert and First Platoon is dealing with demonstrations in Kabul. They're not going to let us go back."

"Why not? We'd go back for you!"

"But they did go back. We wouldn't just have left him there. Lieutenant Kelly made sure they got out there the next morning. He's messed up about this whole thing, too. Todd, buddy, we need you back on the team. You have to get through this or they're going to ship you out for a psych eval. If they do that, it's going to stay on your record and mess up the rest of your career. We've already lost Radar. We can't afford to lose you too."

"How is Mikey?" Todd said looking down at his boots. It was

the first time he'd enquired about the rest of his team since being released from the infirmary.

"About time you asked," Boomer shot back. "He's going to keep his leg but he'll need hip reconstruction. His time with the SEALs is done. Fox is OK. He'll be back in a couple more days—soon as his busted ribs feel OK again." Boomer's voice softened as he looked at Todd.

"It was a tough time out there, Todd. We got lucky. We were only half a step ahead of those guys—maybe less. If Zip didn't track that first group down so fast, Kelly says they would have been waiting to ambush us. We owe a lot to that dog. We all know it, and every one of us is feeling bad."

"Boomer, do you believe in karma?" Todd asked, still not making eye contact with his friend.

"What?"

"Karma—I think what happened to Zip and the rest of us out there was karma. We should have stopped what Hill and Raddock did to that girl back in Kabul and this was our payback."

Boomer sighed and looked down at his boots too. He knew in the back of his mind that he and Todd would have to talk the episode out at some point. "Todd, that was my fault," He said. "I let that happen. In fact, I stopped you from stopping it. I was just so mad and confused when I saw what happened to Wild Bill that I wasn't thinking straight. I wanted someone to pay for what happened to him and she was just there. Plus, we know Hill and Raddock. They're our friends. We've seen them in action before and know they aren't vengeful like that. I guess I just wanted to believe they were right."

"Yeah, me too," Todd replied. "I let you stop me. But we were wrong and karma showed us back in that shitty valley. So, do you believe in karma?"

"No. No I don't. I've seen too much bad go unpunished and too much good go unrewarded for there to be such a thing. There's no balance of good and evil in this world. But I do believe in redemption. The Good Lord will always give us the opportunity to redeem ourselves. We simply need to be ready to take advantage. Now don't tell Kelly I said that. The next thing you know, he's going to be dragging me to church with him."

Todd looked up at his friend and smiled for the first time in the past few weeks. "Thanks Boomer. I'm sorry. It's just that I was supposed to take care of Zip and I let him down. Whatever happened to him out there happened because of me." Boomer opened his mouth to disagree, but Todd cut him off. "Don't say it Boomer—I know. But it's how I feel right now and I just have to work through it. I'll be alright. Let the team and Kelly know that I'm ready."

"That's good, because we're ready to have you back." He dug into his shirt pocket. "And as a reward for being a good boy, you get a Clark Bar."

###

Tajwah Rabbani's cell door opened and Abby entered alone with no escort. He brought with him two comfortable floor mats and an incandescent light with a shade, which he plugged in the wall to give the room a tiny bit more pleasant feel.

"Hello, Tajwah." He spoke to him in Pashto. "Even though you already know of me, I shall introduce myself. I'm Abdul Ashkilani. My father was with the Mujahideen and I grew up fighting beside him. I thought we might talk a while. I brought some lamb, rice, dates, and some cold water. Please, go ahead and eat."

Rabbani hesitated and then looked at the plate of food Abby had set in front of the floor mat. He approached slowly, lowered himself cross-legged onto the mat, looked at Abby with a completely blank expression, and tore into the food.

Abby went on, "I know the mountains and villages well and I understand you are from Khost. I have visited there many times and know the might of the people. It is because of this, I know they will not break you, either."

Rabbani continued to devour the food and listened as Abby went on about the mountains, Rabbani's hometown of Khost, the weather, his admiration for Rabbani's strength, and any number of other pleasantries and small talk. After Rabbani finished, he sat back on the cushioned mat against the wall. He had a feeling of relaxation for the first time in weeks. Abby's droning was almost hypnotic, and the conversation slowly and expertly shifted from Abby, to the mountains and homes, to business.

"Tajwah, we are both Sunni. My dedication is to Allah and I would like to know how we have become rivals."

"You fight for the infidel." Rabbani spoke for the first time. "I fight for the glory of Allah."

"I see. Tell me. How were you inspired?"

The roller coaster ride of emotional and physical stress had weakened him, and the first small feeling of comfort in weeks had lulled Rabbani into a false sense of security. He began to speak without realizing what he was saying.

"Mullah Karmal has the blessing of Allah. His wisdom rivals those of any I have met. He will vanquish the evil doers in our land and usher in a new age of enlightenment. I gladly sacrifice myself for his Holy cause."

Abby quietly listened as Rabbani went on for another twenty minutes, unwittingly doling out information about the makeup of Karmal's troops and general movements through the Hindu Kush Mountains. Finally, Rabbani drifted off to sleep in mid-sentence. Abby looked up at the CCTV camera in the corner and nodded. Staring at the screen in the next room, Agent Kennedy's expression changed ever so slightly. It almost looked like a smile.

The next day, Abdul Ashkilani hitched a ride back to COP Craver Marvel on a supply helicopter. In the middle of the night, he shed his uniform, changed to civilian clothing, and discretely slipped over the wall of the compound—vanishing into the darkness.

###

Zip was still disoriented. Someone had come and scooped him out of the mud. They had cut the tape off his muzzle and, for the first time in days, he could have something to drink. They placed a bowl of food in front of him but he was not hungry. He heard voices and commands swirling around him but none were familiar, and they had given him a shot to make him sleep. When he finally awoke, he was clean and his wounds were bandaged. He could smell the antiseptic stink of the medicine on himself. He was no longer out in the open and there were no chains on him. He was in a cave or some other hollowed out space in the mountains and he was in a cage. A group of men were staring at him as he opened his eyes and rose to look at his audience.

"Well Master, there he is," Abu Habib, Karmal's medical officer, said. "He still needs to eat and the hip needs to heal but I think we stopped any infections from the burns and he looks to be a very strong and otherwise healthy animal."

"He is smaller than the other military dogs, is he not?" Karmal spoke rhetorically, then continued before anyone could try to answer. "Tell Omar Kakur to find batteries for the video camera and prepare a runner to go to our Al Jazeera contact in Jalalabad. Tomorrow, we will show the world our compassion."

###

Todd Mitchell was doing his best to get himself back in shape. Most of the stitches had been removed, and he was starting to feel like his old self. The headaches and sensitivity to light were completely gone, and he was beginning to think clearly again. He focused himself on his training. He had a couple of long Skype sessions with Lindsey back in Pennsylvania and received permission to tell her that Zip was missing in action—but he could not elaborate on the circumstances. Slowly, he was coming to grips with the possibility that Zip might actually be gone and he had to mentally adjust for it like he would over the loss of anyone on the team. He was working out with Boomer and R.J. when Penman came running into the weight room.

"Todd! They need you in the situation room right now! You guys, too," he said as he tried to catch his breath. "It's Zip!"

The four SEALs sprinted for the situation room. When they got there, Commander Heard, Lieutenant Kelly, and Agent Kennedy were staring at the middle screen. On it played a broadcast from Al Jazeera.

"Run it again," Heard said when the other SEALs entered the room.

Someone clicked the remote and the DVR played back. On the screen, a news story began in Arabic, with English subtitles. The SEALs listened intently.

"Today, forces of the Taliban in the Hindu Kush are claiming they have captured a U.S. Special Forces Military Dog. They report that the dog was rescued when retreating U.S. forces abandoned the animal, following an attack on a civilian target in the Perth River Valley that Taliban forces were summoned to defend. The Taliban claim to be treating the dog humanely. This is despite the American Military's repeated use of these animals for intimidation and vicious attacks. They have released this associated video."

A grainy home video popped on the screen. The video obviously had been shot by an amateur, as the camera continually bounced and moved about before focusing on a group of five Taliban insurgents forming a semi-circle around Zip. He was secured with a chain held by one of the men. The men on the screen brazenly clutched weapons and stared at the camera with no attempt to conceal their identities. Zip was shown wearing his ballistic vest, as evidence that it was indeed him, and fresh bandages on his ear and tail were clearly visible. Not much could be seen in the background. There was only a stone wall that could have been the background of a thousand locations. The man in the middle spoke from a prepared script he held in front of him. He spoke in Pashto and the subtitles beneath it were in Arabic. Kennedy translated as the man in the middle began to speak and the camera stayed fixed on Zip.

"Recently, the holy warriors of the Taliban came to the defense of an innocent village being attacked by the forces of the American Military. Through the grace of Allah and the bravery of our fighters, the Americans were driven away and the residents of the village spared. As they often do, the Americans brought dogs to the village to do their fighting. During the glorious battle, one of their animals was unintentionally wounded. The Americans ran without attempting to assist the animal and left it to die. The teaching of the Prophet prohibits cruelty to God's creatures so we have rescued him and he will be well cared for. We have learned that the dog is named Storm. We continue to show the world that we are a compassionate and peaceful people who fight in the name of Allah, and only to protect the oppressed from the infidel crusaders who once again attempt to invade our land. The protection of this animal will be yet another example of our benevolence. Allahu Akbar!" Then, the screen went blank and the Al Jazeera Network went to commercial.

"What the hell was that?" Commander Heard blurted out. "And why are they are calling the dog Storm? Where would they get that from?"

"It's on his vest," Todd answered from the back of the room, still trying to fully understand what he had just watched.

"What?" said Heard.

"His vest," Todd said. "That's the brand name of the ballistic vest he wears—K9 Storm Intruder. They must think the label on the vest is some kind of a name tag."

Agent Kennedy broke in. "It doesn't matter what they call him, only that they gave him an identity. This whole situation is going viral. It's already spreading and has over two hundred thousand hits on YouTube. The spin doctors and media are going to make this thing the top story of the news cycle and it's all going to be politicized. The damn dog is going to have his own Facebook page and Twitter account within an hour." Then she added, for no particular reason, "Anyway, Storm is a better name than Zip."

"So what are we going to do?" Heard asked.

"We're going to end this thing as soon as possible. Give me the remote," Kennedy snapped. She ran the DVR back to the beginning of the Taliban clip. As the camera jumped at the beginning of the segment, she paused it. "See this guy in the background?" She walked to the front of the room and pointed at a blurred image on the screen. "The one with the clean clothes that looks like he's wearing Elvis shades? His name is Nur Mohammad Karmal and he is the ringleader. He's a fanatic and a bad customer and he's probably third in line for the entire Taliban leadership. He's the one that's been terrorizing the villages in the Korengal. He ordered the attack on the COP. He chased your SEAL Team to that old combat outpost, and he has your dog. The guy Kelly's team brought back eventually gave him up. And," she said, in what Heard perceived as a slightly arrogant tone, "within a day or two we will know where he is. When we do, we'll put your team back in place and recon his position. You'll laser target it, and the airstrike will finish the work."

"Airstrike!" Todd jumped in. "What about Zip?"

"What about him?" she responded flatly. "Petty Officer, just what do you think you're going to do? Regardless of what the Tali said on the video, they're going to put a bullet in that dog—if they haven't already. He's nothing more to them than their pawn du jour. They're not stupid enough to think we would actually bargain for him. They plucked the heartstrings of the public today and made it look like the American Military could give a rat's ass about its working dogs. They played the card, and now they're done. Just be satisfied with the knowledge that you'll be there to get your payback."

Todd became infuriated as he listened to Kennedy smugly deliver her monologue. When she finished, he grabbed the end of the folding table he was standing behind and flipped it over, sending it crashing against the wall and onto the floor. Then he stormed out of the room without a word.

Kennedy, as usual, didn't bat an eye but instead fixed her gaze on Lieutenant Kelly. "I did my homework on your boy, Lieutenant. He's a loose cannon and he's emotionally compromised. Now, I don't have any military jurisdiction and can't pick your team but I would say he's a detriment to this mission and should be replaced."

"You may have done your homework on *my boy* Ms. Kennedy, but you obviously didn't do the same research on Zip. That *damn dog*, as you refer to him, saved the lives of half my team while we were being *chased* through the valley. If he hadn't been able to track your prisoner so quickly, we would have been ambushed at Bebiyal and you would be no closer to knowing who this Karmal guy is. Now you've just told Mitchell that he has to go back and place a target on his partner so we can bomb him into oblivion and it *surprises* you that he might be a little upset about that? No, Ms. Kennedy, Todd Mitchell is part of my team and he is coming with us." Kelly looked over at Commander Heard. "Commander?"

Heard was not going to let any spook tell him what to do with his personnel. "That's right. Mitchell is a part of this team and if Lieutenant Kelly says he goes, he goes."

The next day, Abdul Ashkilani returned from his clandestine assignment into the Korengal Valley. "I know where Karmal is," he reported.

Chapter 17
My Loyalty to Country and Team

Commander Heard and Agent Kennedy were impressed with Abby's intelligence briefing. During his reconnaissance, he moved undetected throughout the villages within the Korengal. He triangulated the areas between the COP, Bebiyal, and COP Walker. He used much of the information that Rabbani had unwittingly given him on villages they had visited—those that were assisting the Taliban and those that were resisting. He followed a trail based on the terrain of the mountains and was able to anonymously mix, and discreetly gather further information about Taliban movements by speaking with nomadic herders. Finally, he conducted surveillance around a mountain ridge most likely to conceal Karmal and his men—eventually seeing patrols routinely depart and arrive. He also identified several cleverly concealed sentry posts.

Initially, Heard and Kennedy were skeptical when Abby conveyed his findings.

"Abdul, are you sure? Heard asked. "We have been all over this area. There are literally thousands of drone reconnaissance photographs. We have never found anything even remotely out of the ordinary here."

"Maybe that should have been a clue," Kennedy interrupted, as she munched on a protein bar. "Look at it, Commander." She pulled out a map of the area along with the latest drone photos. "It's quite a place. Look at how there's still trees around the peak and a lot of usable cover. These meadows over here could be the exit area for a network of tunnels that allows them to come and go without drawing attention. This village, here, might not even be a real village—just a front to deflect suspicion."

Heard asked Kelly to comment on the situation after giving him a chance to peruse the information. "Strategically, what do you think Lieutenant?"

"They chose wisely Commander. Depending on where we hit them, they could have a dozen ways out. We'll need to make sure the strike force has bunker busters. Standard high explosive ordnance won't do it. My team is going to need some time to ensure we get a proper target. That means taking Abby with us and moving around the area for a time before we call in the strike. Of course, the longer we're there, the more likely we'll be discovered.

"I recommend that we send in the First Squad initially to do the recon and paint the targets. Immediately after the airstrike, we'll have the remainder of both SEAL Troops and 10th Mountain ready to clear as soon as the Air Force does their business."

"Very well, Lieutenant," Heard concurred. "Kennedy and I will get the plan approved by JSOC. They're already in the loop and only need the details. Begin readying your Team."

Within a matter of hours, Heard and Kennedy contacted the Bagram Base Commander and the Joint Special Operations Command to discuss the operation designated as "Triton's Hammer." The team would almost immediately begin referring to it as "Tri-H." The details were discussed and approved with Kelly, and the First Squad was designated as the insertion team. Once the team located the objective, they would paint the target with a Semi-Active Laser (SAL) homing system. Revolving squadrons of F-16s would be sortied above the area and, when notified, would deliver their ordnance consisting of BLU-109 Penetration Bombs designed to puncture six feet of hardened concrete before detonating their 500 pounds of high explosive. As soon as the F-16s complete the bombing run, ground forces would be flown in from Jalalabad to swarm the area and neutralize the remaining threat.

Once the plan was approved, Kelly met with the squad to brief them on their portion of the mission. The team would be inserted three kilometers from the target at 0200. They would then have time to get to the primary targeting position and begin reconnaissance of the immediate area and determine the optimal targeting position. They would be broken up into two targeting teams and a surveillance team. Todd, Boomer, and Doc Burk would be Alpha. R.J., Penman, and Fox would be Beta. Abby, Angel, and Kelly would be in an oversight and directional position giving cover to both targeting teams. At 0600, the F-16s would be called to make the bombing runs with the remaining ground teams covering by 0615. Kelly's team would then join the arriving ground troops to clear the area and capture any remaining insurgents.

Todd listened closely to the plan. It was simple enough and he was sure that it would be effective when executed. But no matter how much he tried to concentrate on the task at hand, he could not get his mind off his partner who he was sure was still being held alive in the Taliban compound.

He knew that Kennedy was just playing a head game with him by saying they had killed Zip. He wasn't buying it. If they took the time to put the dog on TV, they would keep him around to make another point if it became necessary. The only time they would get rid of Zip was if he became too aggressive, or was holding them up or making noise that drew unwanted attention. He knew Zip was too disciplined for any of that.

His mind wandered as he tried to think of a way he could get to Zip and get him out of there before the airstrike. He conceded, to himself, that it was next to impossible. There was no way he could jeopardize the mission and put the rest of the team at risk. The only possibility was for Zip to create his own opportunity—if he wasn't killed in the airstrike—and get to an open area where he or someone else from the team to could get to him.

After Kelly finished the briefing and they were all back in the barracks, Todd called the remaining squad members together for their own meeting.

"Fellas, I'm telling you, Zip is alive," Todd said, almost pleading as he spoke. "Just like I knew it at COP Walker. What the hell does that spook know? It's just convenient for her to say he's dead—now she can move on with her plan. We can't leave him behind again or just let them kill him. Most of us owe our lives to him. We owe it to him to try."

R.J. saw where the conversation was going and cut Todd off. "Todd, you know how we all feel about Zip, but you also know we can't let that jeopardize the operation. I won't allow you to put any of this Team's lives at risk to try and get him. We don't know enough about the compound or the area."

"I know Sr. Chief. I'm not asking anyone to disobey orders here. All I'm asking is, if an opportunity presents itself, that you give Zip the same consideration that you would give any one of us on the team. This operation is straight forward, but these things are often dynamic. We've all been there—they rarely go directly as planned. If there's a chance, any chance at all, I'm asking you guys to help me take it."

His words hung in the air. The members of the team knew that what Todd was asking was potentially dangerous, not only to them, but to their Navy careers. There was a very thin line here and they all knew that if Lieutenant Kelly even *suspected* that Todd was holding this conversation, he would pull him from the operation and possibly bring him up on insubordination charges. Kelly might even pull the entire squad from the mission.

Boomer moved first. Locking eyes with Todd, he rose to his feet and silently nodded in affirmation. Then each SEAL followed, leaving only R.J. and Todd seated. R.J. looked around the table, meeting each of them squarely in the eyes to gauge their intent. When he was convinced of their resolve, he looked across at Todd and nodded in fidelity.

###

The modified UH-60 Blackhawk helicopter sitting on the edge of the tarmac at Bagram Air Base was nearly unrecognizable. The chopper was equipped with stealth technology that minimized its radar profile and greatly reduced the noise from both rotors and engine. Todd was impressed by how nearly all of the sharp angles were softened and how, other than the whoosh of air caused by the idling engines and rotating blades, barely any sound seemed to be coming from the helicopter. The men of the team boarded the chopper in an efficient, business-like manner and at exactly 0100 they lifted off for the ride back into the Korengal Valley.

There was no conversation as they swept into the Hindu Kush, hugging the sides of the hills. Kelly silently watched each of his men, studying their faces in the dim red light of the helicopter cabin. His gaze lingered on Todd Mitchell, who sat motionless with his eyes closed, and he hoped he had not made a critical mistake by allowing him to join the mission. When they neared the designated landing zone in the Korengal, Lieutenant Kelly moved his hand in a circular motion while holding up one finger indicating to everyone that debark would be in one minute.

The Blackhawk smoothly swept into an open path between the mountains, and hovered twenty feet above the ground. The SEALs connected fast ropes to eyepads welded to the helicopter bulkheads and heaved them out of the side door. Then each man connected carabineers to the line and quietly slid from the chopper into the night. Within seconds of the last man hitting the ground and disconnecting from the line, the chopper pulled up and away from the team. Ten seconds after insertion, there was no trace that a helicopter had been in the area. The SEALs remained frozen as they scanned the landscape with their night vison gear, looking for any sign of movement in the countryside. When they were all satisfied they were indeed alone, they began moving towards Nur Mohammad Karmal's compound.

###

Three kilometers away, a subtle noise roused Abdur Rahman from his light sleep. He stood and walked out into the night air, looking up at the stars and listening to verify whether his ears were playing tricks on him. A lifetime spent in the Hindu Kush hunting and being hunted had given him an extraordinary perception to detect even the most obscure variance in his environment.

In his cage not far from where Rahman was standing, Zip lifted his head from between his front paws, shifted his ears forward and tilted his head to the side as he strained to confirm the familiar sound he thought he just heard.

###

The men of SEAL Team 4 moved through the landscape covering the ground between the landing zone and the objective. The air was still and the sound of each step the men took on the shale stone slope seemed amplified. Kelly was taut as he continually assessed the situation. There was absolutely no indication of any movement around them. There was not a light or a fire in the village they passed, nor any indication of human or animal presence at all. The eventless trek had his mind working overtime. Kelly was beginning to wonder whether Abby had identified the correct location.

As they came up on the place that Abby had scouted, they crept along the outskirts of the small village identified in the surveillance photographs. It was as dead as every other local on the route. When they reached the top of a ridge, Abby called Lieutenant Kelly over.

"There it is Lieutenant. One of the entrances is there, on the right about three quarters up the mountainside. There is no doubt a bunker and cave complex within. I found two other entrances—one two hundred meters farther to the right and another on the other side of the hill. Look, there is a sentry at the first entrance. You can barely see him, but he is smoking."

"OK," Kelly said. "Let's move into our positions. Angel, we need to get to that escarpment up the hill. We should have a good vantage point for both entrances. R.J., get your team's eyes on the entrances we can see. Mitchell, move yours over to an adjacent sightline. We'll target that entrance from both angles. Once you get in position, sit tight and wait until it's time to light this place up. After the first run, shift the target to the second identified entrance. After they pound it, we will bring in the backup."

Just before they all split up, Todd looked at R.J., hoping for some sign of reassurance that he was still committed to the course of action they agreed to back at Bagram. R.J. gave no such indication, but simply spun away and moved towards his designated spot with Penman and Fox. As Todd watched them walk away, Boomer snapped him back to the task at hand. "Let's get going, pal. Pretty soon the Air Force boys are going to be looking for something to do."

Chapter 18
The Full Spectrum of Combat Power

Nur Mohammad Karmal was awake, dressed, and having a cup of tea when Omar Kakur approached him. "Master, Abdur has sent me to inform you. They are here."

Karmal sat with his back to Kakur and did not turn to address him. "Thank you Omar. Assemble the commanders. We meet in fifteen minutes."

When Karmal's commanders gathered as ordered, he welcomed them with his typical blessing and began to explain the reasons behind recent activities at his compound.

"My brothers," he began, "this day will bring great glory to Allah. You are all His holy warriors and we will deal a terrible blow to the infidel—such to the degree that they will certainly withdraw from this valley and recognize that their efforts to suppress us are futile. We will not be merciful. When we have vanquished the devils in our land we will be left to expand His will unopposed and take our next steps to returning the rule of God to all Afghanistan."

He continued. "For the past weeks, a spy has been among us collecting information about our location and operations. He believes he has been discrete and moved among us undetected. He is incorrect. They think they can just drop strangers in amongst us and we will not take notice. The traitor known as the Persian continues to assist the Americans and will soon pay for his sedition. Even now he is with them.

"Their tactics are predictable and arrogant. They rely greatly on their love of technology. We have spotted their advance group and it is now in the process of targeting us. Within the next hours, they will call in their jets to bomb us. When they think they have either incinerated or buried us, they will send troops in to clear what is left. I assure you that their bombs will fall harmlessly. Before their troops arrive, we will eliminate the fools targeting the compound. The arriving troops will come in blind and overconfident, and before they have an opportunity to inflict damage, we will blow them out of the sky and slaughter those that make it to the ground.

"Now, all of you know your positions, so go and prepare your men. Abu, bring the captured animal to me."

Abu Habib had a curious look on his face as he addressed Karmal. "Master, what do you intend to do with the dog?"

"My dear Abu, I am a generous man. I am going to give him back."

###

Todd crouched at his targeting position, his heart in his throat. There was no movement at the compound or any indications that there would be a change in the plan. Although the sun was still ten degrees below the horizon, the sky was beginning to lighten and he began to think of his morning runs with Zip and their time together back at the dairy farm when Caroline was born. He started to break out in a sweat as he looked through the AN/PED-1 Lightweight Laser Designator Rangefinder (LLDR), holding a steady beam on the designated target. Boomer noticed his friend's angst.

"Hey, buddy. Do you want me to handle that? You don't have to do it."

"No Boomer, it's my job and I can handle it. You just make sure the battery stays charged and the cable is connected. It will be OK. But keep a lookout up there. This all seems too easy doesn't it?"

"Yes it does, so far. We'll be done with our part in a couple minutes. Just hang in there."

At 0559, Lieutenant John Kelly made radio contact with the F-16s. "Sierra Tango Two to Falcon Leader, you are clear to make your run."

"Roger that Sierra Tango Two. We have a confirmed target and positive laser signature. Take cover and keep your heads down."

Just as Kelly was acknowledging the message from the F-16 pilots, Angel, who was keeping eyes on the targets through his rifle scope, noticed something. "Lieutenant, the sentries are gone."

And then, the silence of the morning air was pierced with the intensifying sound of Pratt and Whitney afterburner turbofan engines dropping from their designated holding positions into their bombing runs. Todd began to shake, but steadfastly held the laser on his target. Just before the weapon impacts, he silently prayed for forgiveness and for the protection of his friend.

The first two jets dropped the ordnance from twenty thousand feet and swept clear. The bombs self-corrected their course as they descended and homed in on the laser signature. They struck the targets within two meters of the laser point and burrowed into the ground with four, nearly simultaneous thuds. A second later the explosive charges detonated and a rumble began as a gigantic dome of earth emerged from the impact point, followed by a massive explosion as the dome burst spewing dirt and rock in all directions.

"Secondary target!" Kelly ordered without flinching. The two teams adjusted their beams to the second entrance Abby had identified. The second two F-16s made identical bombing runs, and a repeat of the first explosions at the second target left two massive craters where a jagged hilltop had existed just seconds before. As soon as the second series of four bombs exploded, Todd dropped the targeting laser, rolled over and vomited.

"Target destroyed. Thank you gentlemen," Kelly reported to the F-16 squadron. The jets promptly turned and headed back to Bagram. Without missing a beat, Kelly was again on the radio. "Sierra Tango Two to Mike Delta One. Phase One complete. You are a go for Phase Two."

'Roger that Sierra Tango Two. Insertion Team is in route."

"Alpha and Beta Teams, report status," Kelly commanded.

"Alpha all good."

"Beta all good."

Then Abby made an observation that dampened the mood. "Lieutenant Kelly, there's something wrong here. There should have been more movement in this area, even at this hour. When I did my surveillance, there was almost always something going on. Since we landed, we have seen nothing."

"I agree Lieutenant," Angel said. Those sentries were gone before the bombs hit. I think they knew we were coming."

"Everyone remain in position!" Kelly ordered to both targeting teams. "Get eyes on the entire area and let me know if you see anything at all."

There was a long silence and then R.J.'s team reported in. "Nothing here Lieutenant. No sign of wounded or an outside response. You'd think someone might still be alive and looking to see what just happened."

Todd's team echoed the reply, "Agree L.T. It's quiet out there."

As all three groups tried to get a better look the landscape through the lingering dust and smoke of the airstrike, Doc Burk noticed something moving towards them through the debris and in the lightening morning sky. "There's something out there at our ten."

All three positions shifted their binoculars to the spot Doc indicated. It was Angel that recognized the shape first. "Holy shit! It's Zip!"

###

Just minutes before the airstrike, Zip found himself being dragged from his cage and taken to two men. They had been in the circle, taking pictures with him, and in the cave, too. Now they were in another cave, a half kilometer west of where they had been before. His captors left the tape around his muzzle as they fitted him with a new jacket. Zip noticed it was heavier than the ones he was used to wearing. Still, he was glad to be out of that cage.

The one with the sunglasses was speaking. "As soon as the airstrike is over, remove the tape and let him go. He will head straight back to the Americans. Once he gets there, give them your surprise and order the men to attack. Then wait for the other troops and destroy them. If it is possible, bring the Persian back to me alive. If not, try to make his death especially painful." Then, he left.

Zip stood with the one they called Rahman at the cave entrance, looking out into the faint light of the morning sky. The sound of the jets drew his attention and he looked up to see if he could spot them. As quickly as the sound came, it faded. And then

Zip heard the thuds, felt the rumble, and was startled at the sound of massive explosions. Then it all happened again and his captor reached down and cut the tape off of his mouth. It felt good to be able to open his mouth. Then the man smacked him on his rump and Zip jumped out of the cave into the open. He turned to look back, but the one they called Rahman was already gone—vanished into the cave.

Zip stood in the open air for the first time in weeks, trying to acclimate himself to the surrounding environment. It was exhilarating. There was a lot of dust and smoke in the air, but there was something else. He put his nose up, but the smoke made it difficult to smell anything else at all. Then the first scent hit him. Pickles! It was definitely pickles! He tried harder to gather other smells but it was still difficult. Wait, Todd! It was Todd! He was here too! Then, one by one he began to detect the old familiar scents of the rest of the Team—his team! Zip was so excited, he stuck his tail up and moved out at a quick trot towards the smell of his friends.

###

Angel had picked up Zip coming out of the settling dust through his scope and was watching him head directly towards Todd's position when he noticed something. "Lieutenant Kelly, Zip is wearing something. It's a vest … and it's not his normal one." Then he swallowed hard as he recognized what he was looking at. "Lieutenant, he's wired."

Kelly peered at Zip through his binoculars, hoping that Angel was wrong. But there was no mistaking it. Around the entire jacket were pockets packed with what appeared to be small bricks, but were in fact C4 plastic explosive. Coming out of the pockets were wires attached to blasting caps imbedded in the charges. The wires were connected to a radio pack on the top of Zip's jacket that could be triggered by remote control. Kelly nearly choked on the words of his next sentence. "Angel, we can't allow him to get back here."

Kelly said the words before he realized that his communications headset was voice activated and the rest of the team could hear. Seconds later the sound of Boomer's voice broke through. "Lieutenant Kelly, Mitchell is gone."

Chapter 19
The Lives of My Teammates

Zip was still heading towards the scent of Todd, Boomer, and Doc. The clearing air and settling dust gradually allowed his sense of smell to become more acute. As he continued across the open space, another scent suddenly hit him and he froze in his tracks. It was one of the first he was ever taught to detect and it was amazingly strong. Zip couldn't understand why he hadn't picked up on it before. It was the unmistakable smell of cyclotrimethylene-trinitramine—the explosive material in C4. In the cave, the concentration of the chemical mixture was so intense that it had fatigued his entire sense of smell, which explained why it was so hard to detect Todd and the rest of the team when he first left the cave. Now, out in the open air, he could smell the explosive, and he detected that it was all over him. It seemed to be imbedded in his fur. For a few moments, Zip stood motionless, trying to understand what was happening to him. He spun around madly, trying to pinpoint the source of the smell, and quickly came to the realization that *he* was the source. He was danger. He couldn't go towards his team—but now he could smell that one of the team was coming closer to him.

###

Back at the entrance to the cave, Karmal and Rahman were watching, too. "He stopped! Why has he stopped?" Karmal demanded.

"He must know what we have done," Abdur meekly replied.

"That is ridiculous! How could he possibly know? He's a dog! Just detonate the charge and order the men to attack," Karmal snapped.

"Wait," Abdur said. "Where did he go? I don't see him."

All that was visible was a plume of red smoke rising from Zip's last known location.

###

"What the hell is that?" Kelly asked as he saw the red smoke.

"L.T., I don't see Zip anymore," Angel reported.

"Can you see Mitchell?"

"Negative."

###

Even as Kelly finished his comment about not letting Zip get back to the team, Todd had already resolved that he would not leave his partner behind again. He knew what Kelly meant. Before he would allow Zip to get close enough for the Taliban to trigger the vest, Kelly would order Angel to shoot him. He would have no choice.

Todd sprinted towards Zip and as he closed on the dog's position, he knew he had to cover him to delay the Taliban from triggering the device and prevent Nakamura from taking a shot if he was ordered to do so. When he was within thirty yards of Zip, now spinning frantically in a circle, he loaded a red smoke grenade into his FN40 grenade launcher and fired. Then he dropped to the ground, loaded, and fired another so that Zip would be covered from both sides. He ran to the area where the grenades had landed and started searching for Zip, who was nowhere to be found in the thick blanket of red smoke. As the wind shifted and the smoke began to clear, he could just make out the light colored fur on Zip's hindquarters and what was left of the fur on his tail—flying back towards the Taliban position.

###

As the team was searching the smoke, the Taliban opened fire.

The buzz of bullets and sound of the automatic weapons fire was incredibly intense and seemed to come from every direction. RPG rounds slammed into the rocks around all three SEAL targeting positions. R.J. reported in first. "Lieutenant, we're taking fire from everywhere! They've got us zeroed! We're pinned down!"

Kelly was taking the same amount of fire, but was trying to more objectively assess just how bad the situation was. He quickly came to the conclusion that R. J. was spot on and they were scouted the entire time. If he didn't get his team out of there, it would be only a matter of minutes before they were torn apart. He got on the radio to the assault team, now no more than five minutes out.

"Sierra Tango Two to Mike Delta One. Troops in contact. I repeat, troops in contact. The position is not secure and you are coming into a hot LZ. Actual enemy position is one-half kilometer west of original target. We are taking heavy fire and our position is compromised."

Then Kelly gave the only order to his team he could think of. "Engage them with anything you have! There's so many, you could hardly miss!"

###

Karmal and Rahman were pleased with themselves. In a couple minutes the American advance team would be dead and their rescuers would be targeted and destroyed as they made their approach. The carnage caused by the failed attack would surely drive the ISAF from the Valley. "Did you see the dog?" Karmal asked.

"No Master."

"No matter. That was only a bit of flamboyance anyway. Trigger the device and let's be done with it."

"I can't," Rahman replied in a shaky voice.

"And why is that, Abdur?" Karmal said. He still had a crooked smile on his face as he watched the battle unfolding below."

"Because … he has come back."

Karmal's mouth dropped open and his eyes widened beneath his dark glasses as he turned to see the dog, now poised in front of them. Zip's fur was up, pushing through the small openings in his vest, and he was crouched, ready to pounce on his enemy. Karmal and Rahman backed slowly towards the mouth of the cave and as they reached the entrance, Todd suddenly appeared over the rise and began firing. They were barely able to retreat back into the depths of the cave. But Todd stopped. He did not pursue the two Taliban.

His eyes were on Zip and he dove for him, pinning him to the ground. He pulled out his field knife and began to hack at the tape around the remote control device on the vest. But there were just too many layers of tape to penetrate so he started to cut the wires leading to the blasting caps with his knife hand while ripping the caps directly out of the charges with the other. In seconds he had removed almost all of them and cut the remaining wires. As Todd prepared to cut the last lead, Rahman punched the detonator from inside the cave. The blasting cap harmlessly exploded with the force of a large firecracker. Todd found some space below the vest where he could get his knife in without hurting Zip and sliced the vest off. He hurled the entire vest back through the entrance of the cave where Karmal and Rahman had retreated.

"Zip! How are you buddy? What did those sick bastards do to you?" Zip jumped up on Todd elated to see him again as Todd was trying to examine his bandaged tail and hugging him back. "OK, OK big guy. I love you too."

Todd and Zip were now at the entrance of the small cave complex that served as the Taliban command post. He looked across at the various firing positions, daunted by at the punishment raining down on his teammates and friends. He had to do what he could to give them some breathing room before the assault team arrived. Before he could decide upon his next move, Zip was already off and running towards one of the Taliban groups firing on the SEAL positions. Todd bolted after him.

Zip hit the bunker location of Omar Kakur first, ferociously striking the insurgent in his chest and, grabbing the Zarinas from his head, wildly waving his cloth turban like a flag, exposing the position. Seeing that his concealment was being compromised, Kakur pulled out his peshkabz knife and madly slashed at Zip—who gracefully dodged the knife, making Kakur look foolish and making him more frustrated.

Two hundred yards away, Kelly and Angel sensed the slight drop-off in suppressing fire and, for the first time, Angel was able to get into a firing position. He saw Zip engaged with the Taliban and, as he moved to a slightly better position, he was able to properly sight the Taliban and took the shot. A cloud of pink mist burst from Kakur's chest and he slumped to the ground. Through his sight, Angel saw Todd come up on the bunker and covered him as he joined Zip. He watched as Todd took out the remaining two Taliban.

Todd's voice crackled over the comms set. "Lieutenant, I have Zip and we bought you a little breathing room but it won't last long. They look like they are weakest on the right flank. We're going to move on the next two enemy firing positions. When we take them out, that should leave space for Doc and Boomer to get up here. See if you, Angel and R.J. can cover us. What's the ETA on the assault team?"

"Roger that," Kelly said, still a bit perplexed at how Zip and Todd were able to get up and into the Taliban position. "Assault team contact in two minutes."

Todd looked down at Zip. "Now stay with me and don't ever do anything stupid like that again!"

Zip looked back up at Todd and tilted his head as if to say, "What are you yelling at me, for?"

Todd looked for the next target. The firing positions were well concealed and in almost perfect strategic positions. However, they were flawed in a way that did not protect their flanks, and did not easily allow for a clear line of sight between them. Moving quickly, Zip and he could assault each of them nearly undetected. Then Todd saw something else. He could just make out that some of the positions had what appeared to be hand-held surface to air missiles. The Igla "needle" 9K38 man-portable air defense missile had an infrared homing system designed to lock on to the engine heat signature of an aircraft. The armor on the approaching helicopters would be no match for those weapons, and they would be blown out of the sky. There were too many positions and too little time. He had to get his team up for support or there were going to be a lot of dead American soldiers.

Todd had Zip under control now. He ordered him to heel and stay by his side as they moved to the next position, where he was able to launch a grenade into the next bunker area. This cleared a path for Doc and Boomer to catch up to them. The balance of the battle began to shift as the sound of the assault helicopters could be heard thundering into the hills.

Relieved of what had been devastating fire, Lieutenant Kelly was now able to direct the assault team. He instructed the approaching Apache gunships to level the village below them, and the rumble of Hellfire missile hits and chain gunfire echoes told him that whoever was firing on them from that small village was now mortally compromised. It was the break he needed to help Todd and Boomer reach the other SAM sites and allow the approaching Chinooks to put additional forces on the ground. Angel was again able to move into a better sniper position and covered R.J., Penman, and Fox as they headed for one of the SAM sites that Todd pointed out.

R.J., Penman, and Fox took out the site with surprising speed as Angel expediently picked off any adversary lifting his head to view what were quickly becoming less and less offensive positions. Boomer and Doc met up with Todd on the other side of the bunker complex and Todd greeted them. "Glad you guys could make it. I think there's another SAM site over near that next ridgeline. I'll cover you."

When he saw that Boomer and Doc had safely neutralized their objective, he looked at his partner. "Come on Zip, we have unfinished business."

###

The tide was turning and Lieutenant Kelly was able to direct the assault force to a clear LZ. Soon there would be overwhelming force on the ground. The remaining Taliban insurgents were becoming aware of this and were making their personal decisions as to whether they preferred to run or become martyrs. Most were choosing the former. Abby had stuck close alongside Kelly throughout the firefight. When he saw the insurgents begin to flee, he looked at him and Angel. "Come Lieutenant, I know where they are going."

###

Todd and Zip worked their way back to where they had started, and were staring into the entrance of the cave where they encountered Karmal and Rahman. Zip's vest was still where he had thrown it. Todd took a deep breath and said, "Let's go, Zip." As the two entered the cave, Todd was astonished by what he could see. There were light fixtures, computers, weapons, and fairly advanced communication equipment. Sitting next to a pile of equipment was the cage that had held Zip for the past weeks. Todd was hesitant to keep moving inside, but he knew that the maniac that had come up with the idea to blow up his dog was nearby—

and he was not about to let him sneak away.

Zip's discipline and training by now were all back on line. He was in tune with his partner as they systematically worked themselves through the cave complex. Todd shuffled along the labyrinth of connecting tunnels with Zip between his legs and his weapon at the ready. Without a word or other direction, the two SEALs worked symbiotically. When Todd stopped, Zip stopped. When Todd dropped low, so did his K9 partner. Zip had the scent of Rahman and, instinctively knowing that was their target, he cautiously yet deliberately guided himself and Todd towards the intensifying smell.

As the SEALs snaked through the complex, they suddenly came upon Karmal and Rahman, making their retreat. They were gathering or destroying information as they moved through the tunnel.

Rahman saw Todd and Zip first. "Karmal! Go!" he screamed, opening fire on the two SEALs.

Karmal kept moving through the tunnel towards safety as Rahman took a defensive position behind a rock outcropping and raked Todd and Zip's position with AK 47 fire. Rahman was well armed and there was hardly a break in the fire as he expertly changed cartridges and continued to fire. Todd was caught slightly off-guard and, sandwiched in a tiny concave part of the cave wall with very little cover for him and Zip, was unable to return fire. Rahman was relentless and the rounds were taking chunks out of their minimal cover, squeezing Todd and Zip tighter and tighter into the already limited space. No matter how hard he tried, Todd could not shift his body into a position to take a shot without significantly exposing himself. The rounds burst off the rock walls, raising small clouds of debris which pinged off both their bodies. In a matter of seconds their diminishing cover would be completely gone.

Zip sensed Todd's desperation and looked up at him for some sort of direction before realizing he had to make a move on his own. He leapt from the cavity serving as their only concealment into the open to draw Abdur Rahman's attention and give Todd an opening to take his shot. When he did so, Rahman shifted his fire toward Zip who darted back and forth within clear sight. One of the rounds hit Zip near the top of his shoulder, knocking him down.

But in shifting his field of fire, Rahman slightly exposed himself. No sooner had the round hit Zip when Todd spun from his cover and fell prone into the middle of the cave, firing at Rahman and striking him in the neck with a round from his MP5-N. Rahman rose reflexively after being hit and Todd fired another round, hitting him in the right side of his chest. He crumbled against the far wall of the cave.

"Oh no!" Todd groaned despondently as he spotted Zip laying against the wall, bleeding. He ran to help his friend and pulling a gauze pad from the side pocket of his pants, he began to apply pressure to his wound.

On the other side of the cave, Abdur Rahman was bleeding to death. In a last act of defiance, he pulled a hand grenade from his jacket, extracted the pin, and with his final breath, rolled it in the direction of his enemies.

Todd caught the movement from the corner of his eye just in time to turn and see the grenade. He grabbed Zip and picked him up and, as he attempted to spin away, the hand grenade detonated blowing them both unmercifully against the cave wall.

Todd Mitchell was drifting into shock in the Taliban command post with his partner and friend on top of him, but he kept a tight grip on Zip. Doc Burk and Boomer had heard the sounds of the firefight and explosion and came running at top speed. They were unprepared for what they found.

Everything was a complete fog to Todd. He was only making out pieces of what was going on around him. It sounded like Boomer was speaking to him, and he thought he saw Old Doc Burk over him.

"Todd, let him go!" Boomer was pleading with him as Todd kept his grip on Zip's still body.

"Come on Boomer! I need you!" The voice sounded like Doc's but Todd could no longer be sure.

"That's his femoral artery. Put your finger in the hole or he's going to bleed out."

"Who's blood is who's? I can't tell."

"Get his body off of him."

"Oh my God!"

"Stay with me and concentrate!"

"Quick! Wrap his legs!"

Todd's head felt light; he was cold. Then there was silence

followed by darkness.

###

On the other side of the tunnel complex, Lieutenant Kelly and the remainder of his team were heading off the retreating Taliban and rounding them up with the support of the Army's 10th Mountain Division. Abby had directed them to this secondary access point he spotted when doing his reconnaissance. He was scanning the section of the hillside where it sloped and spilled into a meadow when he saw the form of someone slinking out of a small opening; attempting to stay in the shadows of the morning. Abby took off running for the figure and was thirty yards away before Penman noticed and began following.

Abby expertly cut across the sloping ground, staying in his mark's blind spot and closing ground on him. Just as the figure neared the edge of the meadow and tried to bolt, Abdul Ashkilani appeared—seemingly from nowhere—and blocked his path.

"Hello, Nur Mohammad Karmal," Abby said.

"You!" Karmal screamed. "You have assisted the infidel and brought shame to your people. There is a special place in Hell for you."

"I would say the same of you," Abby replied calmly.

"Abby!" It was Penman, who came up on them suddenly.

Abby looked away toward Penman and the momentary distraction was all Karmal needed. He drew a handgun from the vest covering his tunic and fired three shots. Abby's ballistic vest was no defense against bullets fired at such close range and he fell to his knees. Penman continued at a full run directly at Karmal and smashed down on the bridge of his nose with his rifle butt, shattering bone and cartilage and sending his splintered glasses flying from his face.

Penman left the Taliban there writhing in the tall grass and screamed for a medic as he ran to his friend. "Abby! Stay with me! The medics are coming."

Abby responded only by saying the names of his wife and daughters. Then, as blood filled his lungs, he drew one last heavy gurgle of a breath and fell forward into Penman's arms.

Chapter 20
Every Remaining Ounce of Strength

When Kelly learned of Todd's and Zip's situation he worked every angle to get them both taken out on the first available medical evacuation helicopter. Doc Burk and Boomer stayed with them as they lifted off, headed back to Bagram Air Base in extremely critical condition. Then Kelly made the proper arrangements to have Abby's body taken back. Once he was assured his people were well on their way, he turned his attention to his important prisoner.

The moment that Penman had given Lieutenant Kelly the news of Abby and his prisoner, Kelly ordered Penman and R.J. to isolate Karmal back in the cave complex. No one else had seen him exit the caves, or what had transpired when Abby was killed. Kelly told the attending medic that one of the escaping Taliban had fired the shots. He, and what remained of First Squad, were the only ones who knew the whereabouts of the great Karmal. Now it was time to get his first clear view of the legend of the mountains—the man that had caused so much terror.

Looking at the shattered face, and into his empty gray eyes, he was unimpressed. Kelly was in no mood to play games. He had lost a good man and, for all he knew, was about to lose two more valuable and beloved members of his team.

R.J. glared at Karmal, sizing him up. "This is the guy? Doesn't look like much to me. What do you suppose that spook back at Bagram is going to do with him?"

"He's not going back to Bagram." Kelly said.

"Sir?"

"R.J., get on the horn with Leftenant Corrigan at COP Craver Marvel. Tell him to meet us near that first village we passed on the way here. Ask him to keep it quiet."

"Copy that."

"Scotty, you, Fox, and Angel sneak this guy down to that village. Do it in a way that doesn't draw attention. R.J., you and I will get things cleaned up here and meet them in an hour. Tell the Command Center at Bagram we need to be picked up at the COP because we're pursuing some Tali with the SAS—or make up something else that sounds better. I don't care. We'll fly back tonight before dark."

When they all met up and the British SAS transport arrived, Kelly stopped them. "Gentlemen, what I am about to do could end my career. But I am going to do it anyway. None of you have to participate."

Without a question or comment, the five SEALs climbed onto the transport with their prisoner in tow. During the ride, Lieutenant John Kelly stared stoically into space. To the others, he appeared calm and determined. In reality, he was anything but. His hands were shoved down in his pockets. In his left, he painstakingly thumbed each bead as he silently prayed the rosary. He was actually having a crisis of faith concerning the decision he had made.

One hour later, the Bulldog troop carrier pulled up to the edge of the village of Darbat. Kelly asked the Brits accompanying them to wait where they were while his team entered the village with Karmal. As they walked to the center of the village, the tribal elder and other Shuras approached them, curious about this unexpected visit and the nature of their party.

"Penman," Kelly said, "Tell them who he is."

Penman spoke to the elders respectfully and in perfect Pashto, just as Abby had taught him. As he explained to the men about the prisoner's identity, their eyes opened wide when they realized who he was. Their gazes shifted back and forth between the SEALs and Karmal, as Penman told them the details of how he had been captured. Before Penman finished speaking, the elder turned and marched back to his hut. He promptly returned with an Afghan Pulwar sword. It was curved like a scimitar and had a long thin blade that glistened.

Then Kelly instructed Angel and Fox to release Karmal to them. Without a word, the elder and Shuras marched Karmal to a large fallen log not far from where they were standing. The Shuras forced him to his knees and pinned his head to the log. Then, with complete absence of ceremony, the elder raised the blade high above him and swiftly brought it down, severing Karmal's head from his body in one motion.

When it was done, the elder looked up at Kelly with an emotionless expression and nodded his thanks. Kelly returned the nod and the SEALs immediately departed the village. The people of Darbat would burn Karmal's body and scatter his ashes to the wind. The legend of God's Warrior in the mountains was left to fade into the unwritten history of the tribes of the Hindu Kush.

When the team arrived back at Bagram, Agent Kennedy was incensed with the lack of substantial detail about the attack, and the fact that each member of Kelly's team reported that there was no sign of Nur Mohammad Karmal. The intelligence information collected from inside the cave complex yielded no solid evidence of his existence. Nearly all the high ranking individuals who were with him had been killed and the surviving, lower ranking insurgents knew very little of the man. They had seen him but were never permitted to interact. Only a very few privileged individuals ever had access to Karmal. It was as if the man truly was a ghost, and even she began to wonder if he ever existed at all.

###

Three weeks after his arrival at Landstuhl Army Regional Medical Center in Kaiserslautern, Germany, Todd Mitchell slowly began to emerge from a medically induced coma. As soon as he became more aware of his hospital surroundings, he peeked under the sheet of his bed. He saw a bandaged stump near the top of his thigh where his right leg had been. "Oh God," he muttered to himself, dropping the sheet. He sighed and stared at the ceiling. Clarity, and memory, was coming back to him in dribs and drabs.

Maybe he had imagined it. He lifted the sheet again. No, he had not.

Within a couple hours of regaining consciousness, he began to think of Zip. He rang the nurse's station, and quizzed the attending doctors, but no one there was in the business of veterinary care and had no information to give him. Todd was becoming agitated and the nurses were just about to sedate him when Radar Hancock rolled into his hospital room in a wheelchair.

"I hear you're a difficult patient," Radar quipped

"Does that surprise you? How are you Mike?"

"Better than you. I get to keep my leg. I need a new hip but mostly everything else is there. They were just about to send me stateside when I heard about what happened and convinced them that someone needed to be here to ride herd on you."

"Mike, these assholes won't give me any information about Zip. Do you know anything?"

Radar tried to avoid the subject at first. "It was bad, buddy. Your heart stopped out there and they had to bring you back a couple of times in the medevac helicopter. You're lucky you and Boomer have compatible blood types. Doc started a field transfusion before you guys even got off the ground. Those two saved your life a couple of times over."

"Where's Zip?" Todd said through clinched teeth, as if he hadn't heard a word Radar just said.

"Um … he was in really bad shape too, Todd." Radar lowered his eyes to an interesting spot on the floor. "Doc split his time between the both of you. He knew you'd want Zip put first, and he worked on him all the way back to Bagram, and even through the transfer. They flew him up to Landstuhl with you. Everybody did everything they could." Then he looked up at Todd and a sly smile spread across his face. "He's here at Dog Center Europe. It's only fifteen minutes away. They have some of the best vets in the world at the facility in Pulaski Barracks."

An audible cry escaped Todd's throat and he felt hot tears welling up behind his eyes. "Mikey, how is he?"

"He's alive, but still not out of the woods. He was shot above the shoulder in the withers and lost part of the bone. The grenade blast hit him in the chest and front legs. He's lost both legs just below the elbows. He has shrapnel lodged near his heart and he's on his third surgery to try to remove it. The vets can't believe it.

They say he's the toughest dog they've ever seen."

"Yeah," Todd said, wiping a bandaged forearm across his eyes, "he's tough. Mike, please! You gotta get me out of here. I have to see him."

"I had a feeling you were going to say that. I cozied up to a good-looking nurse and a couple of orderlies since I've been here. Get some rest. We'll sneak you out tomorrow night."

Radar arranged the "outing" with the help of the staff he told Todd about. The next night, they discretely moved Todd from his room to a waiting van outside the emergency room entrance and spirited him to the Dog Center. As they wheeled Todd into the room, the sight of his wounded partner overwhelmed him and his chest heaved as he broke down in a sob. Zip lay motionless in what looked like some sort of incubator. There were a number of tubes running from his body, and wires attached to an EKG machine. There were two bandaged stumps where his front legs had been, and his chest fur was completely shaved. Raw stitches ran from below his neck and between his ribcage. It was hard to tell there was even an animal on the bed.

"Zip," Todd's voice shook as he wheeled up to the edge of the incubator. "Zip, it's me. I'm so sorry. This is my fault. You're a good dog. We need you. You can do this."

In his semi-conscious state, Zip thought he heard the familiar voice of his best friend. He shifted his ear to make sure. It was about the only thing he could move. Was it … yes, it was Todd. Then with all the remaining strength he could muster, he lifted his tail and thumped it on the bed.

Epilogue
I Will Not Fail

Recovery from traumatic injury and the associated therapy can be hell. For months after his release from Landstuhl and his return to the Pittsburgh area, Todd Mitchell worked through the physical and mental anguish of adjustment. He was not alone. Lindsey and Caroline were there for him nearly every minute, as well as their extended families. Their presence and support gave him purpose.

Then, there was his special helper. Beside him always, working as a team, was an undersized, banged up, Belgian Malinois-German Shepherd mix with a silly name and a missing ear tip. They received their prosthetics at the same time. Todd's was the latest innovation in titanium and other alloys that allowed flexibility at the joints. Zip's were equally impressive. His prosthetic "legs" and "paws" started just below the elbow joint and were essentially two flexible polymer, diamond-shaped appendages. Where the top leg diamonds met each bottom paw diamond, there was a pivot that acted like Zip's old wrist joint. What took Todd months to get used to, Zip mastered in a matter of weeks. With time, the two would be on their runs again and Zip would catch his Frisbee—albeit at a much slower pace.

Todd eventually returned to school, earning his law degree from Duquense University, and went into business with his father. He would specialize in veteran's affairs, and he and Zip took an active role with the U.S. War Dogs Association and in the Pets for Vets program. Caroline adopted Zip as her own and would welcome him home each day with a huge hug around his neck and joyful screams of "Zippy!" The Mitchell family would grow as they welcomed a second daughter, Abigail. They would call her Abby.

###

Scott Penman was a determined man. For the rest of his tour of duty, he made it his mission to ensure Abdul Ashkilani's family was looked after. He blamed himself for Abby's death and was ardent in his dedication to the memory of his friend. He relentlessly petitioned the State Department to include the Ashkilanis in the amnesty program, and even successfully appealed to the limited sensitivities of Jennifer Kennedy. He contacted Todd, who remembered his conversation with Abby at the COP and appealed to his father for legal advice. Bob Mitchell assisted in navigating State Department bureaucracy. Penman arranged for the assistance of Commander Heard and Lieutenant Kelly to have the women protected and flown to Penman's hometown of Grand Rapids, Michigan, where his family welcomed them as their own.

The Ashkilani daughters adjusted and thrived. Zohal finished school and was eventually accepted to the University of Michigan Medical School. Zahmina Rai would continue to develop her athletic prowess and play soccer at Grand Valley State University. Shaima found channels for her outspoken ways and would go on to fight for women and human rights through Amnesty International and the International League of Human Rights. She would eventually attend law school. Bibi Kur kept a positive face on for her girls. But she would forever struggle with the mental torment of a being a war widow; never really knowing whether the pain and the ultimate sacrifices of her family and husband ever actually solved anything at all.

###

Petty Officer Todd Mitchell was awarded a Purple Heart adorned with a gold star for wounds sustained in combat, and the Navy Cross for valor in the face of the enemy. However, because military working dogs are not eligible for decorations, the Defense

Department would make no official recognition of the contributions of the K9 Navy SEAL attached to the First Squad of the Second Platoon of SEAL Team 4. The team knew Zip deserved better.

The Military Working Dog Teams National Monument stands at Lackland Air Force Base in San Antonio, Texas. When Manny Blanco learned what had happened to Zip, he arranged for a proper ceremony to be held at the monument, where Zip would be awarded a completely unofficial commendation for his heroic actions and his own K9 version of the Navy Cross.

The ceremony was attended by Todd and his family, the men of the team, newly promoted Lieutenant Commander John Kelly, Commander Matthew Heard, Chloe Van Raalten, and some of Manny's veteran military working dog handling colleagues. Zip had no idea what all the fuss was about but he took tremendous comfort in having nearly everyone he ever cared about in one place. He would stand at attention, ears up and forward, as a Marine veteran of the Vietnam conflict named Choatt draped the ribbon and medal over his head.

###

At the small house on the Little R Dairy Farm in the hills of Western Pennsylvania, Zip would spend the remainder of his days with those he loved and who loved him. Each night, when the girls were tucked into bed and Todd and Lindsey were settled down, he would perform his patrol of the grounds—walking the porch and perimeter of the house, stopping occasionally to assess the surrounding sounds and smells. When he was satisfied there were no threats about, the clicks of his carbon-fiber legs could be heard tapping on the wood planks as he headed back through the screen door he learned to open by himself. Finally, taking a position on his bed—strategically placed between Abby's and Caroline's rooms—Zip remained vigilant in the shadow of the hallway nightlight until he drifted off to sleep, resolutely adhering to the fundamental belief of every Navy SEAL.

I humbly serve as a guardian to my fellow Americans always ready to defend those who are unable to defend themselves. I do not advertise the nature of my work, nor seek recognition for my actions. I voluntarily accept the inherent hazards of my profession, placing the welfare and security of others before my own… I will not fail.

Acknowledgements

Nothing I accomplish, from the smallest personal improvement to the most significant milestone, will ever be done alone. I am indebted to the subtle and incisive influences that continually surround me. Without the voices that urge me forward or temper my zealousness, there is no me. I am grateful to my wife and children who help me continually recognize those things in life that really matter, and to my mother, sisters, and late father who have always been my harshest critics and greatest supporters. I am also blessed to be surrounded by the best peer group since the Knights of the Round Table. Without this compelling prevalence, I could never have compiled the words in this story.

Then there are those who humble me every day—those who consciously make the decision to put themselves in harm's way for the greater good. Our military personnel embody the principle of complete and selfless dedication to the protection of the defenseless and the ideals that make us the greatest country on earth. This story is modestly submitted as gratitude for their service and the astonishing contributions of our military working animals.

Made in the USA
Middletown, DE
14 December 2016